The Dark Trails

By William Deek Harris

Antioch, TN 37013

ISBN: 978-0-578-45187-9

Published William "Deek" Harris, Antioch, TN 37013

Printed in the U.S.A.

William "Deek" Harris, November 2018

Cover designed by Illie Dawson

Chapter 1

The Makings of An Outlaw

They say "Two wrongs don't make a right" and nothing could be truer for my lady Bella Rose and me. In our cases it's going to take a string of "wrongs" and even then things would never be "right". No matter how many men we killed, no matter how many slaves we freed, nothing could ever replace all that we had lost. Traveling up and down the trails of the south by night in the early 1800's often proved to be extremely dangerous for most blacks. The paddy rollers were always an eminent threat whether you were free or a runaway slave attempting to gain your freedom; as was the case for my family when we took an ill advised business trip from New York to Maryland. My father had made the trip numerous times with his business partner Jefferson Reed, but never by himself let alone with our family. My father Earl was a knife maker and one of the best in the north. The threat of a civil war raised the demand for better quality weapons. This made my father's company Reed and Black Industries, highly sought after by not only the military but other businessmen looking to get in on the action. It wasn't just their product that was in high demand but their new invention on how to make their knives faster and stronger for less money. Normally Jefferson would have made the trip but he fell ill a week before they were scheduled to leave. My mother begged him to wait until Jefferson was better but he was determined to keep the meeting for the sake of the company's integrity. It was also his opportunity to prove to those white men that he was capable of conducting business alone. Just as determined as he was to go, my mother Mary was determined that he wasn't going alone. That morning when dad got up to load his horse and carriage, he found mom, my little sister Charlotte and I all standing by the door with our bags in hand waiting to load up with him. Knowing that there was no getting out of it, dad loaded us all up and we hit the trail.

The ride was long and brutal but after days of traveling we made it to our destination safely. After two days and two meetings dad decided we would stay an extra night to get more rest. The extra day would not have been necessary had Jefferson been with him. That's because the innkeeper would have allowed dad inside of the inn instead of the horse stable he had my family to make do with. According to the innkeeper he was out of rooms even though Jefferson received a wired reservations confirmation weeks before the trip. The innkeeper was even familiar with my dad on the count of him and Jefferson staying there several times on business trips in the past. That may have been why he at least smiled when he handed my father four blankets and denied us a room then directed us to the horse stable. Needless to say, he still charged the full price of the stay. On our last night everyone fell asleep pretty early and quickly after dinner except for me. For some reason I just couldn't sleep. I wasn't sure if it was the unusual restlessness from the horses in the stable or the bitter January wind whipping through the doors and cracks in the walls of the stable. I heard a thundering sound of several horses riding up to the inn. I peeked through a crack between the doors of the stable to get a glance at who was riding up. There were six white men and one young black male slave. The slave looked terrified and begging for his life. His hands and feet were chained to an unmanned horse. The biggest of the men got off of his horse and walked over to the slave then back handed him for no reason. The slave fell to the ground from the powerful blow and rolled over onto his side crying like a child. But he was no child, young but no child. He looked to be about seventeen or eighteen at the most, which was not much older than I was at the time myself. The big man stood over him and pissed all over the young slave. They all laughed and when he finished the big man walked into the inn but not without kicking the slave in the face to add more insult to injury. I quickly rushed to wake my father to alert him of what was going on. Groggy and half asleep still my father rolled over on his pile of hay and said "Cody you better have a damn good reason for waking me up." I had never been down south or exposed to such a situation. I was at a loss for words and couldn't even answer him. All I could do was point towards the stable doors leading out towards the inn. The look of fear in my eyes spoke more than any words that I could have spat out. In a panic he quickly began to wake up my mother and sister while glancing back and forth at the stable doors. It was freezing cold but sweat had begun to pour from my father's forehead. I had never seen him in such a tizzy. That's how I knew this was serious.

Once everyone was awake my father rushed to the stable doors stumbling and crawling like a bear as fast as he could to see what was going on. He positioned himself behind the stable door then motioned for me to come to his side. "Cody come here. Stay low and keep quiet" he ordered in a whisper only loud enough for us to hear. I made my way to him stumbling and crawling just as he did to get there. He grabbed me by my shoulders and said "They're coming. Take your mother and sister out of the back door. Hit the woods and run like hell. Hide there until morning and have your mother to telegram Jefferson. Tell her to let him know where you are and that he needs to come get you all. She must convince the telegram operator into thinking that she is Jefferson's slave and needs to get home. He will know what to do from there. Do you understand?" I nodded my head repeatedly in agreement although I didn't fully understand at the time. I just knew that I had to do as I was told. "What about you? Aren't you coming with us?" I asked even more afraid once I realized what he was saying. "Don't worry about me. I will catch up with you later. Now go. Quickly they're almost here." I tried to take a quick look out of the crack but was spun around by my father so quickly that I just kept heading towards my mother and sister. In lightning speed I rushed to their sides and relayed my father's instructions. My mother of course tried to resist at first until my father forcefully waved us away and said "Go...I'll catch up with you later." The three of us bolted to the back of the stable for the back door. Just as we got to the door we heard the front doors of the stable fling open and crash against the wall. "Well well well...look what we got HERE Jesse. Looks like it's our lucky day. The keeper wasn't lying when he said he had some runaways out back. I guess we owe that fella a drink." echoed throughout the large stable. It was the voice of one of the slave catchers. It sent a chill down my spine. We could hear my father attempting to inform them that they were mistaken. We stopped and hid behind a carriage stored in the back of the stable so that we could see what was happening. The men were all armed with rifles and pistols on their hips. "I do apologize to you sir but it appears that the keeper has misinformed you. I am not a slave. I have documentation over there in my satchel. I can show it to you if..." my father attempted to say but was brutally interrupted by a back hand from the same big guy that pissed on the slave. My father was no small man and was every bit as large as the devil that struck him. Unlike the slave, my father took the blow and stayed on his feet. He was much stronger than the young slave. My father could have easily tossed him on his ass if he wanted. But it was obvious he was buying time for us to escape. My little sister began to cry so I had to grab her and cover her mouth to keep from being heard. My hands were trembling like a leaf and had to fight back my own tears.

They began to slowly circle my father until they had him completely surrounded. The biggest guy that hit him stood in front of him then said "There's a few things that I hate more than anything in the world. Niggers are on the top of my list. I also hate liars and I know you're lying to me boy. I got a sixth sense for that shit. But I really hate 'fancy dressed and fancy talking' niggers that think some piece of paper is going to stop me from making money off of his ass." My father opened his mouth to speak and before he could get a word out the man said "Ott…I don't want to hear shit you got to say other than where the other niggers are. The keeper said there was four of ya. Where's the other three?" The two of them stood staring eye to eye in silence. My father refused to speak. His defiance outraged the catcher. He slammed the butt of the rifle into my father's midsection and forced him to double over. He stood over my father and yelled "I'm only going to ask you one more time. Where are the others?" Just then I heard "They're right here Paul." The next thing I heard was the sound of rifles being cocked. Standing behind the three of us were three of the six men that rode in with the slave. They came in through the same back door that we were supposed to use to escape. I was so nervous and afraid that I didn't even realize that there were only three men surrounding my dad. "We got em" one of the gunmen alerted to the other three with my father. Together the three of them waved the barrels of their rifles, motioning for us to walk over to join my father. It was clear that they had done this many times before crossing our paths. We slowly raised our hands and stood from our squatted positions. We started walking slowly towards my father then out of nowhere my sister Charlotte took off running to my father. Then a loud thunderous noise rang out over the stable but it was no thunderstorm. It was the sound of a rifle blowing a hole in the back of my twelve year old sister Charlotte. Then another deadly gunshot followed the first and another. Each of them took a shot and tore her poor body open like a bag of wheat. The bullets raised her lifeless body off of the ground with her back arched while her legs and arms flailed in the air. She landed at least three feet from where her body left the ground and crumpled over into a pile of blood soaked hay.

My mother let out a cry like I'd never heard. It was the cry of a woman that had just watched her only daughter's body blown to pieces by the sons of Satan. Her cry was so loud that it pierced the ears of everyone in the stable. In a flash my mother crouched down to one knee and her hand flew backwards. Then I heard a gurgling sound behind me. It was coming from the rifleman standing in the middle of the three. He dropped his rifle and grabbed the front of his neck with both hands. He was trying to pull the small dagger from his neck that my mother threw. From such a far distance away her accuracy was literally dead on. He was gasping for air and tugging at the handle of the blade. The gunman finally managed to pull the blade out. He went from slowly leaking blood to pouring blood from his throat like a water well pump. Everyone was stunned accept for my father. Instead of being stunned, he too quickly went into unexpected action. All of a sudden my father rose up and head butted the big guy in front of him and dropped him like hay from a wagon. While the other two stood in disbelief my father knelt down and retrieved his faithful two shot derringer. He whipped around and put a round in the center of the head of the man to his right. The man's arms flew backwards and his rifle fell to his feet. He dropped to his knees and spilled over to his death.

My father shot at the third guy and missed but the guy was so afraid that he took off running out of the stable. While my father was taking out the three men with him my mother rushed for one of the other two men that were holding us at gunpoint. She wrestled him to the ground and began fighting for all she was worth.. The other man was aiming his gun at me and yelling "Don't move nigger. Don't move!" That's when all hell broke loose. My father took off running towards us to help but before he could reach us there was another thunderous 'BANG'. It was a rifle firing. Again silence and stillness fell upon the stable. It was as though time slowed down and everything was moving in slow motion. I surveyed the stable with my eyes and couldn't believe what I was seeing. It was the body of my beloved mother rolling off of the gunman that she was wrestling. Her lifeless body laid there while her dress soaked her blood up like a sponge. The gunman quickly jumped to his feet dazed at what just happened. Before I could think, I took off running and didn't stop until I was squeezing his neck with both of my hands. He grabbed my hands trying to pry my grip away from his throat but the more he struggled the tighter I squeezed. I could feel the bones in his neck popping between my fingers and I continued to squeeze. Finally he dropped to his knees and his struggle gradually became less affective. I could feel his life literally slipping away in my hands. I realized that for a moment I had blacked out with him dying in my hands. When I had felt him take his last breath it was as though I came back to reality. I could hear my father screaming to me "RUN Cody...RUN!" When I looked up my father was rolling on the ground with the last of the gunmen. He was trying to take the rifle from the man. I looked behind him and the guy he head butted was still knocked out cold on the ground. Again he yelled at me "RUN

SON. Get out of here!" I was confused and didn't want to leave my father by himself. In an instant the decision was made for me. My father had managed to snatch the gun away and let off a round into the stomach of the last devil.

He stood up and held the barrel of the rifle over the forehead of the bleeding gunman. He looked over at my sister then my mother, then back at the man. The man was lying there bleeding and begging "Please don't do it. This wasn't supposed to happen like this." my father tilted his head slightly and said "Yeah I know. You never should have come in here. My family and your friends would still be alive. And so would you." Then he pulled the trigger and opened the man's head with one shot between the eyes. He looked over to me and said "Leave out the back. I have one more to take care of. I'll be right behind you. Now get." He slowly started walking to the last man living, the guy he head butted. I made my way to the back of the stable as my father instructed. I stopped at the back entrance to look back at my father. He was standing over the man and used the barrel of the rifle to tap on the man's face just to wake him. Still woozy the guy held his head up and opened his eyes to find my father pointing the gun in his face. Tears were pouring down my father's face from the pain of losing my mother and sister. My father took a deep breath then wiped his tears with his hands and said "This is for my girls". I turned my head because I had seen enough killing. As much as I wanted them all dead, I just couldn't bear to watch another death. I turned and continued to head out of the back entrance. The sound of gunfire rang out once more. It froze me in my steps as I stood at the back doorway of the stable. I don't know if it was curiosity or instinct that made me turn to look but I did. I couldn't breathe. My heart stopped as I tightly clutched the door of the stable and tears began to roll. I turned just in time to see my father drop the rifle and fall to his knees dead. For it wasn't his rifle that was fired but the rifle of the innkeeper. At least that's who I think it was because he was standing next to the cowardly gunman that my father chased away but he wasn't holding his rifle in the firing position like the innkeeper. Naturally I yelled out "DAD". That alerted them that I was still alive as well as my location. They both began to fire their rifles at me. I turned and hauled ass into the woods. I could hear them chasing me and the bullets ripping through the trees tearing bark away. I barely escaped with my life.

Chapter 2

Falling On Deaf Ears

I ran all through the night only stopping long enough to catch my breath, until I could hear the hounds they turned loose. If I could hear them barking then I knew that I wasn't far enough away and needed to keep pushing to safety, wherever that was supposed to be. All of my life I lived up north free of captivity and never had to deal with anything like this. I had heard of such stories of slaves trying to reach the freedom that I had taken for granted. Stumbling through a pitch black wooded area in search of safety, I quickly learned to appreciate my freedom as it was in jeopardy. It was so dark that I could hardly see my own hand in front of my eyes. The full moon hanging high over my head was the only light that I had to prevent me from nearly running into countless trees. I had left my heavy winter coat back in the stable and the biting cold winter wind was brutally unforgiving. Even with the wind cutting through my vest and shirt as if they didn't exist, I knew that I couldn't stop running or I was a dead man. I ran until I could hear the dogs no more and even then I kept running. My legs were weak and my head was spinning when I stumbled and fell to the ground. I tried to get up but couldn't even muster up enough strength in my arms to push my tired body up off of the ground. I was worn out and too weak to even move. I laid there for a moment to catch my breath since I didn't hear the men or their dogs any longer. I rolled over and realized that I was unable to turn completely over because my shoe was stuck in a hole in the ground. I reached down and was able to feel just how twisted it was, that's when the pain set in hard and fast. I managed to wiggle my foot free from the hole but the pain was excruciatingly unbearable. Again I tried to stand and was able to get to my feet but that was about it. My foot was too busted up to run any further right then. I noticed a huge fallen tree propped up onto another fallen tree with just enough space for me to slide under. I crawled underneath the log and gathered up as many leaves as I could. I covered myself with the leaves to hide my body as much as possible. I tried not to think about the fact that I had just watched my entire family get murdered before my eyes because when I did I would begin to cry. I could not afford to allow my sobbing to get me caught. I had to find a way to get back to New York to my father's partner Jefferson Reed. He was the only white man that could vouch for my freedom since all of our papers were back in the stables. I knew that they would be destroyed as soon as the men got back there and found them. Mr. Reed was the only white man that I could trust right then and I had to get to him.

I woke up the next morning cold, hungry and scared. Not that I was very well concealed by the leaves but obviously I must had completely uncovered myself while I slept. Although it was pretty foggy that morning, the sun managed to pierce through the fog and the leaves. It was glaring down into my eyes making it hard to immediately adjust me eyes but I felt a sense of relief when I focused in on a man that looked to be a little younger than my father's age. He extended his hand to help me up from underneath the log I used for shelter. He was a big man, even bigger than my father and a big smile to match his large frame. I reached out to grab his hand to accept his assistance. His hand felt as large as a dinner plate and rougher than stone. He pulled me to my feet with one strong tug. He was a massively intimidating looking man but his smile made me feel relieved. "What are you doing out here in the cold with no coat?" he asked in his extremely deep voice. We stood face to face but not eye to eye because he was nearly a foot taller than me and I was no short kid at the time. His clothes were old, filthy and riddled with holes. Even the coat he wore didn't appear to be able to fight off much cold if any. But at that moment it was far better than being without a coat at all as I was. He looked like he had to be a runaway trying to also get up north. I figured that we could travel together. A man his size would definitely help if trouble arose. My teeth were chattering and I could hardly speak. I told him "I need help. My family was killed last night at the inn back in town. My mother, father and baby sister are all dead in the stable at the inn. I need to get back to New York and I don't know what to do or how to get there. I don't even know where I am. Please help me." He just continued to smile and said "I got you now!" A sense of security and comfort fell over my body. I was so overjoyed that I grabbed him and hugged him for all I was worth. He in returned wrapped his large arms around my shivering body and held me tightly next to his body. He smelled horrible but I didn't care. I was just glad to see a friendly face with a helping hand, and extremely large hands. My grip was tight but his was much tighter than mine. "HE'S OVER HERE! I GOT HIM BOSS!" he yelled to the top of his lungs. When I tried to release him to pull away his grip became even tighter. I was unable to wiggle my way out of his arms. They were damn near as big as my thighs. My little teenage body was no match for the giant size man. I had been tricked!

About ten white men with guns came running through the fog and trees to see what he was yelling about. The closer they got the louder their celebrating and cursing became. I could hear them coming but I couldn't really see through the thick fog. I struggled to get free but was too weak from hunger to put up much of a fight. Even with a full stomach and full of energy I don't think that I would have stood much more of a chance against the enormous man holding me. Once they were in sight I saw that the mob was led by the innkeeper and the last two gunmen from the stable. They ran up with their guns drawn and surrounded us. The innkeeper and the big guy that my father knocked out walked up closer to us with another man. They stood in front of us and the slave spun me around and forced me to face them. The innkeeper and the other guy were grinning from ear to ear but the gunman showed no signs of joy. The look on his face was cold and heartless. It was obvious that he was not pleased about losing four of his men to my parents and me. "See mister. I told you my brother Charlie's nigger was better at tracking runaways than any dog." the innkeeper boasted to the gunman in charge. The innkeeper's brother turned to the gunman and said "You see, sometimes it takes a nigger to find a nigger. They all know how one another think. You just have to find one that will to do it without getting rabbit and trying to escape himself. But some of them you have to force them. Old Moses here has been tracking niggers for me for about six years now. He's the best I've ever had. So now that we've found your nigger I'd like to get paid so that me and my guys can get out of this cold." The gunman never took his eyes off of me and neither did I take mine off of him. He smirked and yelled out to his other friend "Henry, get this man the money we promised while I take care of this runaway." The very sight of him standing in my face made me feel sick to my stomach. "I'm not a runaway. My family and I were here on a business trip with my father. I've never been a slave. I was born free. Just like all of you!" I pleaded. The innkeeper smacked me in the face and said "You're a liar. I've seen your dad come here in the past with your master. But he must have thought that he could escape and bring his runaway family to hide in my inn. No sir. Not my place he wasn't." I tried to explain but when I opened my mouth the gunman smacked me in the side of my head with the butt of his rifle.

When I finally came to, I was lying on my stomach across the back of a horse with my feet and hands tied together under its belly to keep me from falling off. My horse and I were riding in the middle of the two men from the stable. I had no clue as to how long we had been riding nor where we were headed. All I knew was that I wasn't on my way back to New York. "Mister, I have to take a leak. Can you untie me so that I don't piss on myself?" I asked. They both laughed and just kept riding. "Please, I don't think that I can hold it much longer. I have to go really bad!" I begged. "Hahaha…fuck you! We're not stopping for you. We have about six more hours of riding." the big gunman named Paul answered. "You think we give a fuck if you piss your pants boy? Your whore of a mother killed my brother you black bastard. You can piss and shit your pants for all that I care." the other gunman said. It was the first time that he had said anything to me. He wasn't much bigger than I was and didn't appear to be much older. He was clean shaved with short dark hair. He was the complete opposite of Paul. Paul was a tall man with long stringy blonde hair. His beard and mustache were long and bushy. They covered his lips completely. He looked and smelled as though he hadn't bathed in days. You could probably scrap the dirt from his face with your fingernail. "Don't you worry none Henry, he's going to pay for what they did. He'll get his soon enough." Paul responded to Henry. "You goddamn right he is." Henry said with an evil laugh then spat tobacco spit on the back of my head. For nearly two more hours we rode until Paul had to take a leak himself. They both got off of their horses then walked off of the trail and into the woods. Henry walked on a little further. He obviously had to do more than just take a leak. I could see them both through the trees. I could hear the sighs of relief from both men echoing in the silent woods. "YAAAAH! YAAAAH!" I yelled and began to buck my body as hard as I could to force my horse to run as fast as it could. Not only did my horse take off but so did both of theirs as well. "YAAAAH! YAAAAH!" I yelled over and over. I could hear Paul and Henry screaming for me and the horses to come back. They were running out of the woods and trying to fix their pants at the same time. Henry's pants were around his ankles preventing him from staying on his feet for much more than a couple of steps. Paul on the other hand was in hot pursuit but no match for the speed of a horse. They ran top speed for nearly a mile with me screaming the whole way. They began to slow down and take a drink in a nearby river bank we came to. The other side was way too far to attempt to cross without know just how deep it was and tied to a horse the way I was. My head was hanging over the side of the horse near the bottom of its stomach. I would surely drown before the horse would make it to the other side. I was at the end of the road with Paul and Henry closing in fast.

All I could do was lay there and wait for the inevitable. I knew that running like that was only going to make whatever they had in mind worse than I could imagine. It was only a matter of time before they found me at their mercy. The horse that I was on decided to walk off into the woods to graze on what small patches of grass it could find. I was happy that it did so because it took me off of the main road and gave me some hope that Paul and Henry would not see me. We traveled deeper into the woods and away from the other two horses. They split up and went their own ways as well. Who knows, maybe they were treated as evil as they treated me and if that was the case then I don't blame them. The horse continued to slowly carry me further into the woods searching for food. A rustle in the leaves immediately caught his attention and stopped him in his tracks. He stood still for a moment then bolted through the woods like lightning. I thought that it was Paul and Henry but when I looked around it was a pack of wild dogs on the chase. The horse bobbed in and out between the trees with me bouncing around like a saddlebag. I thought it was the end of us both until the dogs began to drop one by one. I could hear the dogs whimper here and there from a distance. I looked behind the horse and saw a dog topple over and roll several times. When his body came to a rest I noticed there was a stick in its side. I looked over and saw three Indians riding horses with bows and arrows picking the dogs off until the rest decided to retreat. It appeared that I just went from sugar to shit. From the stories that I heard of Indians, they could be worse than slave owners. All that I could think of was that I was going to get scalped and my head set on a stake for display. My heart was racing faster than ever and so were their horses. They quickly caught up with me and slowed my horse down until it had stopped completely. Two of them rode up along side of my horse and grabbed the horse's reins while the third one got in front to assure stoppage. Once the horse was stopped they just sat there on their horses. I waited for them to get off of their horses or something. They never moved or said a word for several seconds. I could hear more horses riding up in a slow trot. It was five more Indians, Only one got off of his horse when they got to us. He walked over to me and grabbed the back of my head and held it up by my hair to get a look at my face. I began praying to God that he didn't scalp me. He said something to the others in his native tongue and they all started laughing. "YAAAAH!' I yelled again hoping the horse would take off like before but he didn't even flinch a muscle. Again I yelled

"YAAAAH!" and again nothing. That made them laugh even harder. I had never felt so hopeless than I did at that very moment. When the laughter died down the Indian holding my head let me go then looked back in the direction of the other four that rode up with them and said something else in their language. He seemed to be the one in charge of them. I was too weak to hold my own head up any longer. I couldn't see everything that was going on but I could hear one of the Indians get off of his horse and seconds later I could hear him walking up. The one in charged kneeled down to where we were eye to eye. He pulled out his knife and held it up for me to get a good look at it. The tears started rolling down my face then I just closed my eyes and prepared myself for the worst. I heard him make a grunting sound and I just knew I was about to feel the pain of his blade slicing through my skin. I was never so relieved when I realized he used the knife to cut the rope under the horse's belly to free my hands and feet from the beast. Then I felt something plop down across my back. It was a heavy blanket from the one that got off of his horse when he was called. I was completely wrong about them. They meant me no harm. Once I was free they both got back on their horses. The one in charged reached down on the side of his horse and grabbed his water container and tossed to me. I was so thirsty that I drank all of it nonstop. One of the Indians beside the one in charge leaned over and said something to the leader. I sat up and positioned myself in the saddle just in case they changed their minds and decided to scalp me anyway. I just didn't know what to expect.

Chapter 3

Tearless Cries

The Indians took me back to see the chief of their tribe. When we arrived we emerged through the heavy tree covers into a beautifully well cultivated land stretching as far as the eye could see. Alongside the land a river flowed with the clearest sparkling water that my eyes had ever seen. The closer we got to the village we were greeted by children of all ages running up to welcome back the warriors. That was the first and only time that I saw them smile or even speak much more than a grunt or two. We reached the center of the village where we were greeted by the elders of the tribe. They led us from our horses and up to a hut that was much bigger than the many other surrounding huts sprinkled throughout the land. The one that cut me loose escorted me inside while the others remained outside and went about their way. We walked in to find five really old men sitting on the ground around a small fire with their legs crossed. They were sharing a smoking pipe that filled the hut with its smoke. They all had large head dresses with feathers that ran down both sides of the back of their heads. The one in the center had a lot more than the other four. With a strong slap in the back my escort forced me to my knees and kneeled before the five with me. He bowed his head until it touched the ground. He slowly rose back up and again slapped me in the back and forced me to do the same. He spoke to the five for a few seconds. It was obvious that he was explaining to them where I came from. The one in the center stared at me without blinking or moving an inch while the other four spoke amongst themselves. He just sat there looking me in the eyes then finally spoke. The others immediately stopped talking to allow him to speak. At the time I had no knowledge of their language.

When he finished speaking the other four began to nod their heads in agreement with his decision. "You are not a slave. Where are your parents?" the old man asked. I was shocked to see that he spoke English. I didn't know if that was good or bad. I was so stunned that I didn't even answer the question. "You speak English?" I asked. He didn't respond to my question but the scowl on his face spoke volumes. "Their...gone...sir." I answered with tears in my throat. The hurt started all over again. I doubled over and fell completely onto the ground and cried for all I was worth. I yelled and screamed "Those bastards killed my family!" The pain of losing my family kicked in so strong that I didn't care about where I was or who heard. At that moment I didn't care if they got upset or scared and killed me also. I just didn't care and couldn't hold it in any longer. The sounds of the words coming from my mouth for the first time, was too overwhelming to handle. They allowed me to lay there and cry until I was all out of tears.

When I was done sobbing the main chief spoke to me and said "I am Chief Long Feather and these are my brothers next to me. Red Bear will take you to get cleaned and some food. You may leave in the morning or you may stay until you are ready to go. I will visit you in the morning for your decision. Now go." He spoke to my escort in his language with instructions. Red Bear stood and grabbed me by the back of my shirt collar and blanket to help me get to my feet with him. He nodded his head and led me back out to our horses. We mounted up and rode through the village until we arrived to a smaller hut but slightly bigger than many of the others that we passed along the way. It was also closer to the water than most of the other huts. Only a few others were the same size or larger and as close to the water. Before we could dismount we were met by twin boys that rushed out from inside of the hut. Red Bear hopped off of his horse and picked up both of the boys. They looked to be about seven or eight years old. They hugged his neck and laughed with him. He put them down then reached into a pouch tied around his waist. He gave each of them something and they ran back inside with smiles. He looked back at me and held his hand up for me to stay put then he followed the twins inside. He stayed inside for quite awhile before he returned with a young squaw following closely behind him. The twins were latched closely to her sides as they slowly walked up to me. "This is Sleeping Flower. She will take care of you until morning. She knows little of the white man's words. I will return before sunset to check on you." Red Bear advised me before mounting his horse. "I didn't know you spoke English also." I said to him but he just looked at me then rode away. Sleeping Flower stood in front of me with her head hanging low with her hands down in front of her. She was a bit shorter than my mother and when she looked up at me my heart stopped. I had seen many pictures of squaws and even a few in person but none as beautiful as she. Her deep black hair was long and thick. It hung down to the top of her waistline. Her copper tone skin was smooth and flawless. Her eyes were as dark as her hair but as soft as her skin. I found myself smiling uncontrollably like a toddler. She gave a little smile back then motioned with her hand for me to follow her into her home. The boys grabbed my hands and happily led me inside behind her. Once I got in she allowed me to bathe and gave me some clothes to put on. They may have been from a family member or lover but I didn't give a damn. I just wanted out of the pissy and shitty pants that I had been wearing for days. When I was done she fed me and the boys deer meat, corn and bread for our meal. After we ate she prepared a spot for me in a corner for me to get some rest while she washed my dirty clothes.

When I awakened from my sleep Chief Long Feather and Red Bear were standing over me with three large warriors standing behind them with spears taller than themselves. I sat up and scurried into a corner like a frightened animal. My heart was racing faster than an angry horse. "Stand up young one. Come!" the chief said then turned and walked outside leaving the others waiting for me to gather myself to join him. I got myself together and grabbed the blanket Red Bear gave me. I wrapped myself up then headed out to the cold evening air. I pulled back the animal skin door to walk out and the bitter night wind smacked me in the face. Everyone was appropriately dressed for the chilling wind except for me. When I got outside I found Chief Long Feather on his horse next to the horse I rode in on. "Where are we going? I asked the chief. Again he grunted

"Come"! Red Bear forcefully nudged me forward towards the awaiting horse. Without a choice I mounted the horse and we all took off trotting towards the center of the village. All sorts of things ran through my mind as we rode. My heart was racing even faster than before. It felt like it was going to jump out of my chest at any minute. Anxiety got the best of me and again I questioned with a bit more force "Where are you taking me?" No one uttered a word. Making a break for it was out of the question. I was surrounded and outnumbered. We came to a stop at the big hut where I first met Chief Long Feather. We walked inside and his four brothers were sitting in the same spot I saw them in earlier that day. "That's him. That's my nigger I was telling you about. Ya see? I told you we weren't lying. Now you can let us get our property and we'll be on our way!" came from the left side of the hut. My head snatched around so fast that I almost broke my neck. It was Paul. He was sitting on the ground next to Henry with their feet and hands tied. "Tell them you are a runaway. Tell em nigger. TELL EM!" Henry continued protesting. The chief looked at Henry the yelled "Silence white man!" He then looked at me and asked "Is what he say true"? The mere sight of the two of them sickened me to my stomach. My rage was building as I stared at the two of them sitting helplessly. "I do NOT know them. They killed my family and are trying to do the same to me!" I responded to Chief Long Feather without taking my eyes off of the two devils. I attempted to charge them but was stopped by one of the biggest warriors in the hut. He stepped in front of me and blocked me with his spear. Red Bear grabbed me by the back of my shirt and blanket again then yanked me to him like my father had done to me many times as a child. He wasn't quite as big as my father but every bit as strong. He pulled me so hard that I fell backwards onto the ground and the warriors didn't hesitate to shove their spears inches away from my face forcing me to stay put. "ENOUGH!" the chief ordered. He then spoke to them in their language and the spears withdrew from in front of my face. Red Bear helped me off of the ground and the chief spoke to them again. I didn't know exactly what he said but the fact that we immediately left and rode back to Sleeping Flower's home made it easy to figure out what he ordered. The same three warriors escorted me back to the hut and didn't leave until I was back inside. It was clear that I wasn't to leave. Sleeping Flower and the boys were still awake when I returned. They looked as surprised to see me again as I was surprised to still be alive. It wasn't much longer before the three of them cuddled up on a large cot. It was made of sticks with an animal's hide stretched out tightly from one end to the other and raised off of the ground. They went fast to sleep once they were settled in. Again I considered running but I had no idea who may had been waiting for me to try to escape. So I laid down and tried to get more sleep. I tossed all night trying to imagine what they were going to do about everything.

Chapter 4

Finding Myself In My Fears

In the morning I was awaken by the feeling of being watched. When I opened my eyes it was true, I was being watched by the twins. I sat up and stretched to awaken my limbs with the rest of my body. Multiple nights of sleeping on the ground was beginning to take its toll. I was really missing my comfortable home and bed back in New York. Sleeping Flower was heating up some food in a skillet over an open fire. The aroma drew something from me that hadn't happened in awhile, a smile. She acknowledged my smile and returned the gesture. I got up and walked outside to take my usual morning piss. There was no designated outhouse that I saw so I decided to head to the water to relieve myself. The morning air was cool but I figured I could make it to the riverbank and back before I froze. Just as I began to head for the water I felt a hand on my shoulder. It was Sleeping Flower with a winter coat in her other hand. "For you!" she said as she extended the coat for me to take. It was the first time that she had said anything in English and her voice was as beautiful as her face. I smiled and accepted the generous offering. It fit perfectly. It was a heavy long overcoat made of bison hide. The arrow hole in the chest area of the coat led me to believe that it once belonged to someone killed by a warrior and brought back to the village. I didn't care though. All that mattered was that it fit and was serving its purpose. I thanked her for the coat and headed for the water before I pissed in my pants again. As I walked I admired the beautiful sunrise's reflection dancing on the water top. The closer that I walked the more mesmerized I became. So much so that I tripped and fell over something on the riverbank. I nearly swallowed my own teeth when I glanced back to discover that it wasn't a rock or log but the bodies of Paul and Henry. They were buried standing up in a hole up to their shoulders. Their head and shoulders had been mutilated to nearly beyond recognition. If it hadn't been for some of Paul's beard being still attached to the bloody and mangled skull sticking out of the ground I wouldn't have been able to tell who was who. There was no question as to how they got there but what I didn't know was why they were there. I needed to see the chief and fast. I needed to see if I was next. I hurried to my feet and took off running for Sleeping Flower's home. When I got there I rushed inside where Sleeping Flower and the boys were standing in a corner with their heads down. The boys were standing in front of Sleeping Flower with her hands on their chests with them held close to her. I glanced over to the left where my blanket and sleeping area were to see Chief Long Feather and Red Bear standing there. "I see that you have found the white men that chased you. You not have to worry no more." said Chief Long Feather. My jaw dropped wide open. "Come, walk with me." he commanded. He walked up to me and put his arm around my shoulder and led me outside.

We walked out to the river's edge where the remains of Paul and Henry stood out of the ground like ravaged meat flowers. The ground surrounding them was soaked with their blood and chunks of flesh scattered around the human stumps. We got within feet of the bodies before I froze up and couldn't walk any longer. "What did you...why? Why did you do this?" I asked. I couldn't stop looking at how destroyed their bodies were but couldn't go any closer. The chief stepped in front of me to shield my young eyes from the horror that unbothered him and Red Bear. There was no telling how many times they had done this or worse to men. "How old are you?" the chief asked me. "I'm sixteen. Well that's what my parents told me. I don't have any official papers anywhere that I know of. Even free blacks are no concern to white folks enough to keep records like that." I answered. The two men looked over at one another and both nodded simultaneously. "What do they call you?" the chief asked in his less aggressive tone than most of the others. "My name is Cody…Cody Black." I answered. "Those men were evil. My warriors found them wandering around the woods. They have killed many Indians for long time. The spirits led you here for us to find them. Many families will have some peace now knowing that the wolves have fed on them after the bison had their daily morning run on the water side. You too can now have peace." Chief Long Feather informed me. I didn't know if I should be relieved or sad. Just the thoughts of being trampled by a herd of bison and then eaten alive by a pack of wolves, was bone chilling even for them. But then I thought about my baby sister, my father and beloved mother and I was glad they died a brutal death. The chief put his arm around me again and we headed back to the hut. Neither of them uttered a word during the walk back and neither did I. I was still in shock and wouldn't have been able to say anything even if I had something to say. I then knew why many people both black and white feared the Indians. My grandfather on my father's side was full blooded Cherokee but I never met him. My father didn't speak of him much. My dad was the closest I had come to knowing an Indian but that didn't really count to me. He was nothing like the stories of Indians that I had heard. Although he didn't speak of my grandfather much he always taught my sister and I to treat everyone with respect as long as they earned it. We got back to the hut and Red Bear mounted his horse and waited for Chief Long Feather to have another word with me. The chief stood in front of me and said, "Cody we are proud Shawnee Indians. Before the white man came we had many villages throughout the land. My village is the last of its kind. Each of my brothers had their own village before the white man burned them to the ground and killed many of our people. Together we are stronger. Alone we are like sitting rabbit for hunter. You are safe here and welcome to stay and live as Shawnee lives. Or you may go and find your own way. The choice is yours. I will send for you after the sunset. Then you decide." He turned and walked off to join Red Bear. They rode off without looking back and I went in to join Sleeping Flower and the twins. I spent the better part of the rest of the morning trying to wrap my mind around all that had happened in just a few days. Regardless to what I decided, my life as I knew it was never going to be the same.

The twins were really beginning to warm up to me and so was Sleeping Flower. The twins taught me several little games to play to pass the time while Sleeping Flower left to go to the village. After a few hours had passed she returned with a sack over her shoulder. She sat it on the floor and the boys rushed over to tear into the sack. It was filled with fruits, vegetables and a chunk of meat. She stood over the boys and smiled at how pleased they were with the food she provided. She looked over at me and extended her hands towards the food and said with a smile "Eat. Is good for you...eat!" I was starving and didn't hesitate to jump down on the ground to join the twins. As hungry as I was I still allowed them to pick first then quickly snatched up two apples and sat in my little corner on my blanket. I gobbled them both down so fast that I barely tasted them. When I finished I looked over to find Sleeping Flower and the boys sitting around the bag. They were looking at me and giggling. She tossed two more apples over to me and I devoured them just as quickly as the first two. After a long day of playing games with the boys my energy level was all but gone. The apples provided a much needed source of energy. After everyone had finished eating Sleeping Flower nestled up on their cot for a nap. The boys and I played a few more games but it wasn't much longer that the three of us were tired as well. I took a seat on my blanket and spilled over from exhaustion but with a smile. The boys thought that it was hilarious. They sat next to me and mimicked my display of fatigue. Instead of joining their mother on what was surely a much more comfortable sleeping arrangement, they bunkered down next to me on the ground. One of the boys grabbed a large animal skin just before we all laid down. The three of us used it to cover our bodies while we slept.

Night soon fell and Chief Long Feather sent Red Bear to come get me. The boys were still asleep but I heard Red Bear enter the hut and so did Sleeping Flower. We both sat up as he stood in front of the entrance. He looked over to me and said "Come!" then walked back out. Slowly I got up carefully trying my best not to wake up the twins. I grabbed the coat that Sleeping Flower gave me and headed towards the door. Before I could get outside Sleeping Flower rushed over to me and grabbed my hand then said "The boys like you and you are kind to them. I hope you come back and stay." Her voice was soft and soothing. "Must go now!" Red Bear shouted from outside. She released my hand and walked over to where the boys were then laid down next to them. I turned and hurried outside before Red Bear called for me again. We rode off and headed to the meeting with the chief. Red Bear wasted no time and pushed his horse to the limit. I didn't want to get left behind so I followed suit and got low on my horse to gain more speed. I caught up with Red Bear in no time. We raced our horses as fast as they could run glancing over at each other. I caught a glimpse of Red Bear smiling. I don't think he expected me to be able to keep up but I was no stranger to riding. My father and I used to race each other to the house from our favorite fishing hole every since I was big enough to get on a horse. We arrived to the meeting hut with me edging Red Bear out by two horse lengths. When he came to a stop he looked over at me with an evil glare that slowly turned into half of a smile. I knew then that he was just testing me. We walked in and Chief Long Feather along with his brothers, were all sitting in their usual spots on the ground. The chief extended his hand towards the ground for me to have a seat across from them. A circle of large stones enclosed a small fire that separated me from them. The familiar aroma of their pipe filled the air as it had the last two times I was there. I took my seat across from the men and patiently waited for one of them to speak. After a moment of awkward silence I finally asked the chief "Are you going to say anything?" He looked on both sides of him at his brothers then began to chuckle. It didn't take long for his brothers to follow suit. They laughed so hard that even I had to giggle a little, especially when I looked behind me and saw Red Bear laughing as well. Finally I asked "Ok...so what's so funny?" Chief Long Feather looked across the fire and said "I am not the one that needs a home. You are the one that has to let us know what you have decided. You are free to go or you can stay. If you go, you have to decide where will you go? If you stay, you stay and live as a Shawnee." At that moment it all became surreal to me. His words spoke volumes because he shed light on my dilemma. I had no more family. My mother was an only child and her parents were hung by a lynch mob when she was a child. She escaped and fought her way to freedom alone as a teen until she met my father in New York. My father's parents were both gone and his only brother died from pneumonia long before I was born. It was the first time that it actually hit me that I was alone in the world and literally had nowhere to go. I started thinking back on the night that I lost my family. The pain of the memory hit me like a bag of rocks. The tears began to build and my heart felt torn to shreds. Before I knew it I was balled up on the ground crying my eyes out. I could barely get the words "I want to stay" out of my mouth through my snot and saliva choked voice. I didn't really want to stay but I felt as though I didn't have any other option considering the alternative was to head out into a cold and evil world that I was obviously still learning. I was neither prepared nor capable of surviving on my own and I knew it. To leave would have ensured me a life of slavery or worse…death. From my account death would have probably been better than slavery but I wanted neither. I was allowed to lay there and get it all out. Then I felt a strong consoling hand on my back comforting me and ensuring me that I was in good hands. It was Chief Long Feather's hand. "Stand up young one. Everything will be ok. You may go back to Sleeping Flower and my grandsons' home. I will send for you again tomorrow." he stated. I made it to my feet and received a much needed hug from the chief. I was still pretty torn up and too weak to even return the hug. The comfort of his strong arms reminded me of hugs from my father that I would receive no more.

Chapter 5

Growing Up Shawnee

I spent the next couple of years learning and living life with the Shawnee Indians. I continued to live with Sleeping Flower and the twins Screaming Eagle and Roaming Cloud. They taught me the Shawnee language and I helped them and many others with their English. With the approval from Chief Long Feather, I was accepted by the tribe and I was grateful. On my eighteenth birthday I was sent to the woods to spend seven days alone to show bravery and to become a man. The night I returned, the tribe prepared a huge celebration as they did for all of the young men coming into adulthood. The river bank was lit up with torches and large fires. Chief Long Feather brought me before the tribe at the edge of the river. He and I stood waist deep in the warm water along with Red Bear. The chief raised both of his hands high above his head. In the Shawnee language he loudly announced "Tonight the spirits are pleased once again. Tonight…I…am pleased. The boy that once entered our village as a scared child has grown into a mighty Shawnee brave. If anyone does not agree, speak now and challenge Cody." I don't know if it was the 'I dare someone to say something' look on Red Bear's face or the fact that I had grown into a six foot three mound of a man but no one moved a muscle. The chief waited a moment then lowered his arms and placed his right hand on the top of my head then began a melodic Shawnee ritual chant. When he finished the night air was filled with celebration cries from hundreds of Shawnee. We all celebrated and rejoiced over my induction into my new family. There were people everywhere eating and dancing along the river bank. I sat with the chief and his brothers while we ate and watched everyone. Although I was now a part of the Shawnee tribe I couldn't help for thinking of my family looking down over me. It was as though I could feel their spirits hugging me. The feeling became so overwhelming that I needed a moment to alone. I excused myself and walked off until I was out of sight of the chief. I slipped into the woods and found a tree stump to have a seat. I sat there thinking of all of the memories of my family and how things would have been if they were still alive. I could still hear my little sister's laugh and see my mother's smile. I longed to hear my father's voice once again. The memories cut through me like a knife and dug a hole in my soul that would never be filled again. The tears began to run like the river and onto my shirt. They smeared the markings Red Bear painted on my face for my ceremony.

The sound of my own sobbing must have drowned out the sounds of footsteps approaching me from behind. A light touch on the back of my shoulder alerted me that I was no longer alone. It was Sleeping Flower. I was unaware that I was seen leaving but pleased to see her warm smile. She slowly slid her hand from the back of my shoulder, up my neck and gently wiped the tears from my eyes. Her touch was nurturing and very much welcomed. She told me not long after I moved in with her and the boys about how their father, Moon Bear died from fever years before I came along. He was the also the son of Chief Long Feather. His mother, Chief Long Feather's wife was an African woman with a rich dark complexion like my mother. From the descriptions I heard over the years, Moon Bear was a dark mixture of both of his parents much like my father and I. So I knew that she could relate to the pain of losing a loved one but not her entire family. "Why do you cry? You are a man now. Are you not happy?" Sleeping Flower asked in a comforting voice. "Yes I am very pleased to be welcomed into the Shawnee family but I miss my first family" I responded with my head hanging low. She raised my head with the tip of her finger and said "They will always be with you Cody. Their spirits will live in you forever." She grabbed me by the hand then pulled me to my feet. "Come with me." she suggested and I followed. Together we walked deeper into the woods until we could no longer see even the flicker of the flames from celebration fires. We walked until we came to an opening through the trees that led to a cove with a waterfall as high up as the treetops. The full moon hung above the waterfall, beaming off of the sparkling river water. Its glow lit the area almost as much as the fires of the ceremony. "Follow me!" she demanded then released my hand and jogged off down the side of the river. Her elk skin dress bounced back and forth with her two ponytails trailing down her back. When she got closer to the waterfall she ran into the river and began swimming towards it. I jumped in and followed behind her. She swam out into the middle of the river and waited for me to catch up with her. The water glistening on her face and hair was mesmerizing. She reached out her hand for me to grab then pulled me in close to her. It was the first time that we were able to be eye to eye without me stooping or sitting. Even in the moonlight I could see her beautiful dark brown eyes looking through me. "Race you to the waterfall." she suggested then disappeared under the water to get a head start. I could hear her giggling as she pounded the water. I took off right behind her. We reached the waterfall and I was amazed at how beautiful it was up close. Sleeping Flower emerged from the waist deep water and headed for the waterfall. "Come on. You are slow like old man" she said looking back at me. I could have beaten her to the fall but the view of her backside moving in the water was more rewarding. So rewarding that I was unable to rush out of the water without her seeing just how much I enjoyed watching her. Unfortunately the water still wasn't high enough to hide the huge erection I had. Watching her running in the water was not helping my situation any. She stood under the waterfall and allowed it to pour down onto her body while she held her head back to receive nature's bath. She reached her hands out inviting me to join her in the water. I did as she wanted and accepted both of her hands. She pulled me in close and wrapped her arms around my neck. She looked up into my eyes and asked "Have you ever…you know…been with a woman before"? My heart started pounding like a war drum. I closed my eyes and slowly shook my head no. I was too ashamed to bring myself to say the actual words. She reached up and pulled my head down to her then kissed me. When we finished we stared into each others eyes for a moment. Sleeping Flower turned and disappeared behind the waterfall. The water continued flowing into a cave concealed by the overflowing water rushing down from high above. I followed her into the cave and walked up behind her. I put my hands around her waist and she began to grind against me. Slowly she raised her wet dress above her hips exposing her perfectly round cheeks. Her skin was soft and smooth. I pulled my pants down to my knees where the water stopped. She placed her hands on the wall of the cave and allowed me to make love to her. I walked into the cave a boy but I left as a man!

Chapter 6

When Morning Came

Every day I learned something new from the Shawnee. Over time I learned to hunt and fight like them as well. My father taught me how to handle a knife but the Shawnee warriors taught me how to master it. The tribe was heavily stocked with an assortment of spears and blades but a very limited supply of firearms. The few that were available were mainly obtained from the aftermath of conflicts with white soldiers or some shady trade arrangements. Chief Long Feather made sure that I was given my own pair of Colt .45 pistols to wear on my hips. Red Bear had taken me under his wing and became my mentor. Actually he was more like a father figure and Chief Long Feather was like the grandfather I never had. They accepted me for who I was and never tried to change me but I embraced the Shawnee life with everything in me. I was always allowed to wear what I wanted instead of the traditional Shawnee clothing. There were clothes from deceased white men but I refused to wear any of them other than the coat Sleeping Flower gave me. I lived as a Shawnee, so I dressed as one. Sleeping Flower continued to teach me sexual lessons over the next couple of years. I had not become just a man, I became her man. I was

69

really concerned that Chief Long Feather would not agree to us being a couple, but to my surprise he not only welcomed the idea he demanded that we eventually get married. Although I was concerned about the chief, I was even more concerned about how the twins would feel about it. I was even more pleased that they approved and welcomed the idea as well. However, Chief Long Feather did have one demand and that was for us to have a traditional Shawnee wedding. I was fine with that considering I hadn't seen many other weddings to have any expectations for my own when the time came. The twins were becoming of age and their quests to become men were scheduled only weeks away before our wedding was scheduled. Sleeping Flower wanted to wait until after their achievements. She didn't want our wedding to over shadow their time. When the time came they both set out to the woods alone just as I had done a few years before them. Their test was a bit more challenging than mine because it was winter when they left. Two days into their ritual we had one of the heaviest snowfalls of the season. If they had been any other kids I would have been concerned. But they were grandsons of Chief Long Feather. They had been taught and trained by the best warriors in the tribe. They knew everything about how to survive off of the land. On the night before they were to return Sleeping Flower informed me that we were going to have a child of our own. Just the thought of having a child filled me with pride. Sleeping Flower and I took advantage of our time alone to celebrate by making love all night long.

The next morning we woke up to the sounds of the village in an uproar. Before we could get out of bed to see what was going on Red Bear rushed in and yelled "Come to the village. Come quick." Then quickly he darted back out. I rushed to the door just in time to see him on his horse racing off but not in enough time to ask what was going on. We hurried to the village on our horses as quickly as we could. The closer we got to the center of the village where the chief normally met we had people rushing up to us in tears. We rushed inside looking for Chief Long Feather and the others as well as Red Bear. But we were not expecting to see the bodies of the twins lying on the ground with their heads sitting next to them. Sleeping Flower's cry out was as deafening as my mother's was when Charlotte was shot in the stable. She dropped down to both knees and buried her face into the dirt crying the tears that only a mother could cry. Slowly she crawled up to their headless bodies and threw her body across them with her arms stretched out to embrace them both. I was frozen stiff with shock. I inched my way over to her and kneeled down to comfort her as best I could. Nothing could ease the pain that she was experiencing but still I held and caressed her broken hearted body. She turned to hug me back and planted her crying eyes in the center of my chest. I looked up at the chief and asked "What happened?" The look of pain was deeply set in everyone's face but none more palpable than Chief Long Feather's. Without saying a word the chief reached across the lifeless boys' bodies and handed me some papers. The top page was a letter in a handwriting that was barely legible. The other papers were official government documents with 'The United States Congress' printed at the top. "What is this?" I asked. "It was with the horses they were tied to when they got here. It is written in the white man's language. I am able to speak their language better than I can read it. I need you to tell us what it says. I know that it will tell me who did this to my grandsons." he answered while fighting back his tears. Sleeping Flower could no longer stand anymore. She jumped up and ran out crying.

I stood and walked closer to the door so that I could get more light to read the papers to the chief. It says "You are being sent these official orders from the United States government but this letter is from me, Col. Wayne B. Johnson of the United States Calvary. You have three days to pack your things and get the hell off of our land. You can go peacefully or you can go the way these two animals went. Anyone that resists will die!" The rest of the papers were government papers saying that the Shawnee had to move to an Indian reservation hundreds of miles away. Even if we were willing to leave, three days was not nearly enough time to pack up an entire village and be moved before they came. "What do you want to do?" Red Bear asked with both fists and teeth tightly clinched together. The chief never looked up from gazing at his grandsons but simply responded with "I have a burial ceremony to plan. I need everyone to leave my brothers and me to make plans." Red Bear attempted to speak again but was cut short by Chief Long Feather barking "GO!" at us all. We all did as ordered and exited the hut before upsetting to chief any further. When we got outside, Red Bear huddled up with a group of warriors. I moved in closer to join in so that could better hear the conversation. The crowd grew larger and louder as everyone was chiming in to offer their suggestions. The majority was for striking out looking for the white men to attack before they could attack us. The rest of the crowd was either willing to wait on instructions from the chief or willing to do whatever. "SILENCE!" Red Bear screamed and silence was given. "We are all angry and upset. None more than me. I too want to go out and seek revenge. But our chief, in his great wisdom has asked that we allow him time to plan the burial of our beloved little ones. We must respect his wish and await his orders. For over thirty years he has led us and not ONCE has he failed us. We cannot fail him. We must wait and allow him to lead us in what to do next. And we must trust that his decision will be for our own good. I…trust in him. You…must trust in him as well. Go to your families and inform them that we will wait on our chief's orders. The white man is sneaky and can't be trusted. Arm yourselves and your families for any sneak attack from the white man. Now go, we have two of our young ones to honor tomorrow." Red Bear announced to the crowd. The crowd dispersed and everyone went their separate ways as suggested. As everyone was leaving Chief Long Feather stepped to the door of the hut and called for me to come back inside. I rushed over to see what he needed. He said "Cody I need you to read to me and explain every word in the rest of the papers. It is a must for our people that I have a clear understanding of everything on the papers."

After hours of reading and explaining the papers I discovered that it wasn't just our tribe that was being run off of our land. The government basically decided that they needed the Indians' territories for their own settlements. They marked off a small section of land west of the Mississippi River for hundreds of tribes live. Anyone that resisted would be forced off or killed. The tribe had been on the land for nearly a century and was not leaving without a fight. That night Chief Long Feather called for war council in the big hut with his brothers and the strongest warriors to discuss their strategy on how to defend their land. Most of them wanted to strike out for the woods to hunt down the army and take the war to them. The chief felt that would be too reckless of a move. It would cost too many lives to rush into the woods without knowing how many men they had or their exact location. We were even unaware how long they had been out there watching and planning an attack. There were just too many unknowns that could leave the rest of the village extremely vulnerable if the mission failed. Instead of rushing in blindly to a potential slaughter, the council agreed to send three men into the woods under the cover of the night to scout out the army and report back what they saw. In the morning the burial ritual for the twins would go on as customary. The scouts were to return as soon as they got as much intel as possible. The expectation was for them to return before sunrise but if they were not back before the burial ceremony then we were to assume that they were captured and to prepare for immediate war. Once the decision was made, Chief Long Feather ordered the scouts to head out for their recon mission. The rest of us were ordered to return to our homes and to spread the word for everyone to meet at the burial grounds at sunrise. He also asked that everyone pack up all of their valuables that they could carry and bring it with them to the burial grounds.

Chapter 7

Blood and Fire

In the morning everyone got up at sunrise and gathered their things just as the chief ordered. We all met up to say our final goodbyes to Screaming Eagle and Roaming Cloud. The burial ground was placed up high on a stretch of land across the river that overlooked the mouth of the river. In order to get there we had to cross the river then climb the steep river bank hills. It was the sacred grounds that their ancestors and loved ones had been buried on for years. A pile of large flat rocks were stacked up high above ground level. In order to be heard by the masses, Chief Long Feather often used it to stand on and address the tribe. After the ceremony he took his place on the rock platform for all to hear his words. He looked out over the crowd then said "Today is a sad day for all of us. Today I had to do something that no man or woman should have to do. We all know who are the cause of our sadness today. We all know that they are here to do what they did to my grandson to all of us. They have stolen from us, raped and killed our women and children. They have done this to our people for many moons. They are here now to continue their evil ways. They want us to leave the land that we have lived on for longer than even I can remember. I asked you to bring your valuables with you for a reason. Late last night the scouts returned with the location of the white man's army of hundreds. The white men have their own lookouts watching us. If they saw everyone packing things and leaving then they may think that we are giving in to their demands. It will also keep them from being destroyed should the white men find them. They have no idea that Red Bear and two hundred warriors surrounded their camp just before sunrise. I have spoken to Chief Big Bull of the Cherokee through the drums and smoke signals. We have put aside our differences for the sake of our people. They have two hundred more warriors joining Red Bear and the others to help defend our lands. Most of the warriors that are not with Red Bear will return back across the river with me to join the battle and defend our home. The women and children will stay here on this side where it is safest. Red Bear and the others should be starting their sneak attack any time now. We will NOT give up our land without a FIGHT!" The crowd erupted in cheers and war cries. Before we left to fight I asked the chief "Why didn't you let the rest of us know?" He put his hand on my shoulder and said "I had to make it look like the entire tribe was coming. If only the women and children came then they would have known something was not right. That's why I only sent half of our braves to join Chief Big Bull. The white men may be evil but they are not dumb." While trying to console Sleeping Flower during the burial ceremony, I completely overlooked the fact that Red Bear was nowhere around but it all made sense.

Over a hundred of us all hurried back across the river by horseback. The galloping beasts trampled through the river splashing so much water in my eyes that it was hard to see. We arrived at the village to find it undisturbed still. But on the other side was the roaring noise of war in the woods. Guns were blazing and the sound of death rang out over the trees. We raced through the woods as fast as our horses could run. We reached the battle and were met with a shower of bullets from the trees. Warriors were dropping all around us but that didn't stop us from charging in with rage in our hearts and weapons in our hands. The warriors that had rifles returned fire that cut down the first line of defense for the army. That allowed us onto the battlefield for war! From the number of dead and injured soldiers on the ground, it was obvious that Red Bear's attack caught many of them off guard. But as many as there were on the ground there were just as many Indians there as well. The only problem was that there were still more of them alive than us...hundreds more. Chief Long Feather and I rode into battle side by side. He yelled over to me "Stay with me. We need to find Red Bear." He knew that I had never been in battle but my years of training prepared me well. I had never killed anything more than the animals that we hunted for food but when a soldier came running up towards us with his sword, I didn't hesitate to drop him with my pistol before he got close enough to swing his blade. There were individual fights all around us as far as the eye could see. As we rode through the clashes the chief drew his tomahawk and sliced up any soldier he could reach from his horse's back. To save my bullets I followed his lead and began to do the same until my tomahawk got stuck in the top of someone's head. I lost the grip and was unable to pull it out before my horse forced me to release it still in the man's forehead. My bow and arrow skills were not quite as sharp as most of the other warriors. The chief was aware of this so he tossed me his tomahawk to defend myself. Then one by one he began picking off soldiers with his bow and arrows. I, on the other hand continued chopping away at any nearby man that had white skin.

Finally through the crowd we spotted Red Bear in a distance on the ground wrestling with a soldier. We rushed as fast as we could to give him help but kept running into more and more white men to kill. With Red Bear in need of help I slung my tomahawk into the chest of the closest soldier that I could find in my path. Then I pulled out both pistol to clear a path to my mentor. My first bullet blew the top off of the first guy. In the corner of my right eye I spotted my next victim. I opened his stomach with two shots back to back. One after the other the chief and I took out as many of the soldiers as we could until we could get a clear visual on Red Bear. He and the soldier rolled around several times making it hard for me to get off a shot without possibly hitting Red Bear. They came to a stop with Red Bear on top with his hunting knife in both hands hovering over the soldier. The soldier was holding Red Bear's hands and fighting to keep from being stabbed but he was not strong enough to save himself. Down came Red Bear's blade, piercing the soldier's face. His lifeless hands immediately dropped to the ground. Red Bear stood over the dead soldier facing us and raised his blade high in the air. I knew then that he saw us as well. Then he fell over face first onto the ground. The top part of his head shattered from a rifle bullet at close range. "Noooooo!" both the chief and I yelled. The soldier that shot him was even younger than I was but that didn't matter. I knew that he was nervous from the way he was just standing there looking in shock. He noticed that I was racing straight for him with my horse. I ran out of bullets but wasn't going to let that stop me from charging him with my horse. He raised his gun to shoot me but an arrow from the chief penetrated his chest before I could reach him and before he could get off a shot. He dropped his gun and fell to his knees trying to pull the arrow out of his chest. I ran my horse right over his body before he could succeed. The hind leg of the horse crushed his head into the ground when he fell over. I hopped off of my horse and rushed over to his dying body. I got on my knees next to him and finished bashing his face in with the butt of my pistol until his face was gone. I looked over and found Chief Long Feather cradling Red Bear's body. I ran over to them and wrapped my arms around the both. The pain of losing more family drove me to tears. The chief looked up and looked around the battlefield at all that was going on around us. He said "Cody you must go and warn the others. There are too many of them. Soon they will take over the village and find the others." "And what about you?" I asked. "I must stay here and continue to fight. Now go please. You are their only hope. GO" he responded with tears in his eyes. Reluctantly I did as asked but I felt it meant that it would be the last time I would ever see him again.

I was able to make it on the other side of the fighting without any altercations until I got to the very edge of the opening leading to the village. There was a soldier that must have spotted me running through the trees and decided to follow me. I didn't even know that he was behind me until I heard "Stop nigger or I'll shoot!" I stopped running then slowly turned around. "Where do you think you're going?" he asked pointing his rifle at me. "What the fuck is a slave doing out here fighting with these redskins? I guess all of you savages are the same anyway." he said walking up to me and cocking his rifle. My heart dropped to my stomach and I closed my eyes then prepared myself for the blast. No sooner than I closed my eyes I heard the rifle fire but I didn't feel anything. When I opened my eyes the soldier was standing even closer in front of me with the rifle still pointing at me. I looked past him and saw Chief Long Feather lying face first on the ground with his bow and arrows lying next to him. Behind him was another soldier. From the looks of it the chief was going to shoot the first soldier before he could shoot me but got gunned down before he was able to get his shot off. I couldn't believe what was happening. The first soldier had turned his head to see what happened but before he could turn back around I snatched him close to me and dug my knife deep into the side of his neck. The other soldier fired a shot at me. I used the dead soldier's body to shield me from the bullet. Quickly I grabbed his rifle and returned fire dropping the second soldier before he could get off another shot. I ran over to the chief and rolled him over. He looked up at me and said with his last breaths "Find Sleeping Flower and save yourselves. They have already started burning the village." I looked over through the trees and he was right. I could see the smoke and flames consuming the village. When I looked back at him his eyes were closed. And just like that, he was gone!

I could hear the sounds of the battling quickly moving towards the edge of the woods. There was no time for mourning the loss of the chief if I was going to make it to the others in time to warn them. I looked through the trees and the chief was right. They had already begun to burn the village. The thick black clouds of smoke stretched high above the trees. I gently kissed the chief on the forehead and placed his head on the ground. I ran as fast as I could to the village. I got to the closest hut and hid behind it to see where the soldiers were. I could hear them but I couldn't see them. From hut to hut I hid until I was close enough to get a visual on a group of soldiers on horses riding through the village with torches. They were riding around setting fire to everything. A few of the warriors that were left behind had come to attempt to fight them off but were unsuccessful. They were all slaughtered like animals. A group of them were heading across the river to seek out and execute the remainders. I ran around the side of a burning hut and found an unsuspecting soldier on a horse with his back to me. Slowly I crept up behind him and snatched his ass off of his horse. Over and over I pounded my fist into his face until he was either unconscious or dead. I quickly took his two pistols and jumped on his horse then raced towards the river. I was spotted by one of the soldiers in the village. He chased after me but not for long. I turned and put a slug in his chest to stop him. He fell off of his horse and I continued chasing his friends through the river. They were way too far ahead of me to get off any good shots. I rushed up the hillside behind them in hot pursuit. Unfortunately they were not the only ones that had the same idea. There were many soldiers already on the hill before them. By the time I reached the top of the hill where the others were, I was too late. They had already massacred the entire tribe, women and children included. The tribe that had become my new family was wiped out by the white soldiers. It was the second time white men had claimed the lives of my entire family. I reached the burial grounds just as the soldiers were heading back off to rejoin the battle they were ruthlessly winning over the tribes.

I got off of the horse and dropped to my knees crying uncontrollably. Most of the tribe was gunned down in cold blood with no regard. Many were mutilated by the swords of the soldiers. They spared no one, not even the babies. I sat there for a moment wondering how anyone could be so cruel and ruthless. I found my way to my feet and wandered about the slain bodies looking for Sleeping Flower. When I found her she had been shot several times, as many of the tribe was. The woman that I loved and carried my unborn child had been senselessly taken from me for no good reason. My hatred was magnified from that point on. Outgunned and outmanned, I found no reason to return to the battle that would surely claim my life as well. I sat on the ground holding and rocking Sleeping Flower's limp, blood drenched body as I watched the bellowing smoke from the fires claim the only other home that I knew. At that moment I realized that white men had taken away everything and everyone that I loved from me. I vowed to myself to return the favor.

Chapter 8

Best Served Cold

For the next year or so, I lived off of the land in a small hut I built several miles away from the condemned village that I once called home. I isolated myself until I was fortunate enough to come across a stroke of good luck. I was out one morning checking my rabbit traps when I heard the sound of horses pulling a stagecoach with two men sitting up front. I hid behind a tree and watched. The driver was a small well dressed white guy with glasses. The other guy was much bigger but I couldn't see him very well. The coach came to a complete stop. The bigger guy got off and walked around to the side of the coach to where I couldn't see him any longer. He opened the coach door and a white woman in a blue dress got out to stretch her legs. The driver hopped down and opened the other door for two other well dressed white men to get out as well. The bigger guy stayed on the other side out of my view. I carefully moved from tree to tree to get in a little closer for a better look. The two men walked on the other side of the coach and off the trail into the woods to take a leak. The lady and the driver were the only ones that I could see. "Oh hurry up. We're going to be late fooling with you two. I told you not to have so much beer before we left." the lady yelled at the two men as she paced back and forth with her arms folded. There was no telling what was on that stagecoach or who they were but I was going to find out. I waited until the two men were deep enough into the woods before I made my move. The driver was standing guard and cradling his rifle like a newborn baby. The bigger guy was still on the other side out of sight. So I walked out from the trees with both pistols drawn. Before either the driver or the woman could say anything to alert the others I placed the barrel of my pistol to my lips to give them the hush sign. The driver knew that I had the drop on him so he wisely set his rifle on the ground. I motioned with my pistols for them to get closer and walk to the other side of the coach so that I could use them as leverage against the other three men. The big guy on the other side was finishing up from taking his leak when we walked up behind him. The other two men had their backs to us as well but were only a few feet away. I had the drop on all of them. The big guy was the first to turn around and show his face. I couldn't believe it when our eyes made contact. It was the slave Moses that helped Paul and Henry capture me when I was sixteen. Before either of us could say anything, one of the other two men turned around. His head was down focusing on fixing his britches and talking to his buddy. "I can't wait to get there. I'm going to…" he started saying just before he looked up and found the barrels of my guns pointing at him and his friends. He reached over and patted the other guy to get his attention. "You better be glad I was finished. Because if I had pissed on myself…" the other guy started to say until he also discovered the shit they were in with me and my guns. I thought that I was happy to see Moses but I was even happier to see that the first guy to turn around was the innkeeper and the other was his brother.

I lined them all up against the side of the stagecoach at gunpoint. "Well…well…well look at what we have here. It's like a reunion." I said with a laugh. "You won't get away with this nigger!" the innkeeper shouted at me. "Do you know who you are messing with?" his brother added. "You will hang for this. You black nigger!" the brother continued. I walked up to the innkeeper and stuck the barrel of my gun under his chin and said "Who's going to stop me motherfucker?" Then I moved over to his brother standing next to him and asked "Who the fuck is going to hang me? And call me a nigger again. I dare you!" His face turned beet red and shouted "Who the fuck do you think you're talking to BOY?" That's when I shot him between the eyes. The lady started crying and freaking out because his blood and brains were all over the side of her face. The innkeeper started yelling "But he didn't call you a nigger!" Then I shot him in the face also and said "No but you just said it." The stagecoach driver bent over for his rifle on the ground so I put a bullet in his back that went clean through his heart. Quickly I turned my attention back to the lady and Moses. "Now that the business has been handled, let's have a little fun. Moses why don't you find some rope and tie this bitch up for me? Then you and I are going to have a little fun." I demanded. The lady got even more frightened and screamed "Wait...please. Please don't rape me...PLEASE!" Over and over she kept begging not to be raped. Moses kept standing still as though he hadn't heard a word that I said until I pointed my pistol at him then cocked it and slowly said "Don't make me have to tell you again." He could tell from the look in my eyes that I was not playing. He stepped up on the coach and grabbed some rope. "Now tie her hands to the stagecoach door and step away from her." I ordered. He tied her as he was told and she would not stop screaming. I holstered one of my pistols then reached down and snatched the pocket off of the coat that the innkeeper was wearing. I walked over to her to check the rope and made sure it was tied tight enough to keep her from escaping. Then I stuffed the pocket in her mouth and shoved my gun barrel under her chin then said "I don't want to hear another word from you. And I don't want any of your white ass. Now sit here and shut the fuck up before I come back over here and blow your damn head off. You got that?" She stopped crying but began sniffling and nodded her head to let me know that she would do as told.

I turned and faced Moses with only a few feet of space between us. "So you don't want to rape her. Now what?" Moses asked looking confused. I put my other pistol in my holster then took my gun belt off and laid it on the ground next to me. I took off my jacket then said "The last time I saw you I was still a child. You deceived me and made me believe that you were going to help me. Then you turned on me for what, these two?" I said then pointed at the two dead brothers. "You sold out your own kind just so that you can get a pat on the back by some motherfuckers that hate you. What now you ask? Now I'm going to kick your ass. Then I'm going to kill you!" I continued as I began to slowly walk up to him. He just smiled and said "So you got it all figured out huh? You want to kick my ass? Let's do it then!" He charged me and tried to bear hug me like before. I ducked and scooped him up in the air. I held his large body over my shoulder then fell forward and slammed him to the ground. I fell on top of him but he managed to flip me over and gave me two of the hardest punches that I ever felt to my ribs. I reached up and dug my thumbs up his nostrils and tried my damndest to rip his nose off of his face. He didn't waste any time getting off of me. It was a technique that Red Bear taught me when all else failed. We both got to our feet as quickly as we could and put our fists up. Again he rushed me but that time I shot a left jab to his right cheek then a right hook to the side of his huge bald head. It felt like punching tree. My punches staggered him backwards a few steps but that didn't stop him from coming back with three of his own punches. His blows did more than stagger me. They knocked me flat on my ass but not out. Moses came running for me full speed but again Red Bear's training came in handy. I tripped him up with my feet and forced him to ground level with me. I jumped on his back and wrapped my arm around his neck and locked it in with my other hand. The more he squirmed the tighter I gripped him. "Wait…wait! Let me explain. I had no choice. They were going to kill my family! I had no choice!" he pled gasping for air. "Don't kill me please!" he continued to beg. "Why should I believe you?" I asked then wrenched down even tighter on his neck. "Because I can make you a rich man. I have a plan. Just listen to me please!" he argued for his life. Part of me wanted to snap his neck but more of me wanted to hear about how he planned to make me rich. Slowly I began to loosen my grip. He had tricked me once so I didn't let go completely until he started talking. "You see that pretty little white woman over there? That's Miss Hannah Starr. Her family is rolling in money and they don't trust banks." he said. "And what does that have to do with me?" I asked tightening back up on his neck. "The innkeeper was her stepfather. He has been sneaking into her room every since she was a little girl and her mother allowed it. You killing him makes our plan even easier to carry out. If you help us there's more money in it for you than you'll ever see out here in these woods." Moses said gasping for air once again. And once again I loosened my grip. But when I looked up into the white woman's eyes I could tell that he was not lying. I released Moses and jumped to my feet as fast as I could, leaving him still on the ground caressing his neck. I grabbed my gun belt off the ground and pulled one of the pistols out and walked over to Moses. I pointed the barrel at his crotch and said "If this is another one of your tricks to try to get a reward for bringing in another slave…" I cocked the hammer of the gun and advised "I will blow your balls to hell!"

Chapter 9

The Plan

Moses and Hannah stayed with me in my hut for the night while we discussed the plan they had already devised. Now that I was a part of the equation we had to make a few modifications. I found out a lot about both of them that night. I learned that Moses was forced into slave hunting by the innkeeper and his brother. In fact the innkeeper was as broke as I was until he married Hannah's mother Scarlett. Scarlett was married to John Starr, the heir to Starr Paper Mill. He opened the inn for Scarlett as a means of providing her with a sense of purpose. John passed away from a heart attack when Hannah was only ten years old. Two years later Scarlett got remarried to Richard Hill, the innkeeper that I killed. Less than a year into their marriage Richard began sneaking into Hannah's bedroom late at night and having his way with her while Scarlett slept. With no siblings to confide in, Hannah turned to the only other person she thought would have her back and protect her. But it was useless; Scarlett would dismiss Hannah's accusations as childish fairytales and lies. As time went on she realized that her mother not only wasn't going to protect her but that she wasn't always asleep either. Time had not been kind to Scarlett. Her figure had become more robust and skin not as tight any longer. She knew that she was no longer the young perky breasted young lady she once was when John was alive nor when she met Richard for that matter. Eventually his actions became more and more blatant until Scarlett began to encourage it just to keep Richard around. Scarlett's suggestions that Hannah accept Richard's advances forced Hannah to develop an equal amount of hate for both her mother and Richard. On Hannah's eighteenth birthday Richard brought a surprise home for her. It was his brother

Charlie. He told her it was time that she became a "real" woman and that was his gift to her. That night they shared her while Scarlett remained in her room listening to Hannah's cries for help. This became a regular weekend event for years. Hannah became their own little sex toy. She was denied the privilege of seeing any other men or anyone for that matter. They kept her in the house most of the times except for when they went on trips like the one they were on. She was their insurance to a guaranteed good time while away. In many ways she had become their slave in her own rights.

For Richard's generosity with Hannah, Charlie offered him a couple of his own slaves in return. He also included Moses and his family as part of the package as long as he could use the services of Moses whenever he needed or wanted. Moses was purchased by Charlie when Moses was a young man at the age of twenty six. He bought Moses from a tobacco and corn farmer name Elijah

Stokes. Elijah couldn't seem to control Moses. Moses had escaped four or five times from the Elijah's plantation. Charlie discovered that Elijah also owned Moses' wife and two children. Initially Elijah only wanted to sell Moses but Charlie made him an offer that he couldn't refuse. Charlie offered not to tell Elijah's wife about the affair he was having with her sister if he sold the entire family for the price of one. Reluctantly Elijah gave in to Charlie's blackmail tactics for fear of divorce and public ridicule. Charlie forced Moses to help him track and capture other slaves for other slave owners for a healthy fee that many were more than willing to pay. Business was going great until one day Moses decided to rebel and run. When he was caught Charlie forced Moses, his wife and his five year old daughter watch his seven year old son hang to death. I sat and watched the pain and tears in Moses' face as he told me "That devil told me 'I'm doing this now because I'm not going to put up with what Elijah dealt with. If you run again I'm having that nappy headed bitch that gave birth to him hung from the same tree then I'm going to let the boys turn that other baby monkey into a real woman. She would have more baby monkeys than you can shake a stick at. Then string her up when I'm done with her. You got that boy?' I wanted to kill him right then but I knew that if I tried then my son wouldn't have been the only one I lost that day." That's when I was convinced that they were telling the truth. Those sick bastards got exactly what they had coming to them but that wasn't enough in my opinion.

Moses and Hannah planned to kill Richard and Charlie while away on their so called trip to purchase more slaves. The plan was for Hannah to give them the night of their lives, get them drunk then kill them in their sleep. They agreed to say that the newly purchased slave stole a gun and killed them both before running away. Then they were going to kill Scarlett once the shock of losing Richard and Charlie died down around town. They didn't want things to look too suspicious. Richard didn't believe in keeping their money in a bank. After he convinced Scarlett to sell the paper mill he became really paranoid over the money. He didn't trust banks with their money. He convinced Scarlett to keep all of their money in a safe hidden in the library of the plantation. Once Scarlett was gone then they could split the money up and go their separate ways. Their plan sounded good but it had some holes in it that would have gotten them both killed. More importantly I wasn't about to wait all of that time. I didn't give two shits about what the town thought or things settling. I spent the majority of the night learning as much as I possibly could about the plantation and who all were there. If this was going to work we were going to need help from the other slaves on the plantation. Scarlett wasn't expecting them back for a few more days. That gave us time to sneak back onto the plantation and speak to some of the others. The biggest concern was going to be Jacob, the plantation's overseer. He wasn't a very big man from the way they described him but he was quick tempered and whip happy. They said he loved to patrol the plantation by horseback cracking his whip just to see the slaves shake in fear. At anytime and usually for no reason there were at least two whippings weekly from his evil hand. He was the true definition of a cracker, riding around cracking his whip. According to them he even had many of the other white men afraid of him as well. Everyone feared him, including Richard and Charlie. With thirty plus slaves and less than twenty plantation workers Jacob ran them all single handedly with a whip. I couldn't wait to meet him!

The next morning I woke them up before sunrise so that we could get an early start to the plantation. Moses and I loaded the stagecoach then the three of us struck out leaving my little hut behind. I decided that since we had a little time to burn that we would stop in town and spend the night at the inn Richard and Scarlett owned. I hadn't been back there since the night that I lost my family. I also hadn't slept in a real bed since the night before we left our home in New York to take the trip to Maryland. According to Hannah it wasn't uncommon for her to be at the inn with Moses standing guard over her while Richard was around town chasing more skirts. When we got to the inn Hannah convinced the innkeeper that I was one of their newly purchased slaves and that Richard was out celebrating. She had him to give her two rooms, one for herself and the other to keep the new slave, me supposedly tied up until morning. He gave her the keys for the two rooms and we headed up the stairs to get some rest. On the way up the stairs we were met by an old, short white man with a thick white beard. I could tell that he had plenty of money by the way he was dressed. He was escorting a much younger black woman. I had not seen anyone as beautiful since Sleeping Flower. As beautiful as Sleeping Flower was this woman was absolutely stunning. Her skin was as golden as fresh honey. Her eyes were hypnotizing and her smile was inviting. As they passed the couple nodded to us to say hello and kept on down the stairs. Our eyes locked onto one another's. I couldn't take my eyes off of her. She looked back up the stairs at me and gave me an even bigger smile. It tangled up my feet and I tripped going up the stairs. The old man looked back to see what was the commotion behind them. Hannah quickly went into character saying "You clumsy nigger! Can't you even walk a flight of stairs?" Then she grabbed my arm and pulled me to my feet. It took all that I had not to knock her damn teeth out but instead I grinned and went up the stairs. The old man smirked and they went on about their business. When we got to the room I had them to tell me more about the layout of the plantation but not before I let Hannah know that I would break her jaw if she ever talked to me that way again. I learned everything that I needed to come up with the perfect plan but I just couldn't stop thinking about the lady on the stairs. She wasn't dressed quite as fancy as the old man but she definitely wasn't dressed like a slave. Her hair and skin were way too clean to be a slave.

Chapter 10

The Thorn Of A Rose

During my long overdue nap I was awakened by a knock at the room door. Startled and discombobulated I quickly snatched my pistol from under my pillow and aimed it at the door. I cautiously approached the door with my pistol in hand ready for whatever. "Who is it?" I asked in a low voice. It was Hannah and Moses. I allowed them to come in before someone saw them and got suspicious. "You interrupted my sleep!" I growled at them both. "Yeah well we're going across the street to the saloon to get a bite to eat. Are you coming or staying here sleeping the night away?" Hannah asked me with a little coy smirk. Normally I probably would have told her no but out of the corner of my eye I saw the same woman from earlier through the window. She was by herself this time and headed across the street to the saloon Hannah was talking about. The twist in her hips made her dress bounce back and forth from behind. I had to see her. "Yeah sure, I could use something to eat. Let's go." I suggested. Hannah looked at me side eye and walked over to the window. She moved the curtain back with her hand to get a slightly better view outside. She turned back to me with a grin then slowly walked up to me and said "Oh I see what you have an appetite for but if you know what's good for you, you might want to look at something a little less fattening on the menu. Besides, everyone knows that white meat is better for you than dark meat and tastier. Ain't that right Moses?" Then she whipped around for his response. I glanced over at him as well and a look of embarrassment covered his dark face. He never uttered a word but instead hung his head in shame. "Well personally I find white meat to be a little TOO dry for my taste. I prefer something juicier and with a little more meat on the bones too, if you know what I mean." I responded then gave her a little slap on her flat ass to further emphasize my point. She attempted to slap me back in the face but I quickly caught her hand before she could touch me. Hannah glared into my eyes and said "You think you're so tough don't you? Well go right ahead. Her name is

Bella…Bella Rose. Don't let the pretty face and curves fool you. She's as mean as she is pretty." Little did she know but that made me want to meet this Bella Rose even more.

We walked over to the saloon and before we could get through the door it flew open. An extremely dirty white man came staggering through the door. He tripped and grabbed onto Moses to keep from falling. It was clear that he had way too much to drink. When he realized Moses wasn't a white man like himself, he forcefully pushed himself off of Moses and said "Get your nigger hands off of me. You filthy animal!" He hocked and leaned back to spit on Moses but Hannah stepped in front of him to stop him. "Don't you dare!" she told him. The man looked her up and down then staggered away mumbling "Fucking niggers are taking over this city." Hannah looked down and saw that I had my hand on my gun and said to me "You're going to have to either get rid of that thing or give it to me. It's bad enough that you aren't dressed like a slave but that gun is going to get us killed." I got as close to her as possible and said "Let's get something straight. Right here and right now! I'm NOT a slave! I never have been and never will be. And I'm NOT about to even pretend to be one. And the next time you ask for my gun, I'm going to give it to you alright. One bullet at a time." Moses chuckled at the look on Hannah's face. She whipped around to Moses and responded with "You need to wipe that smirk off of your face because you sir are a slave." I snatched her by her arm and pulled her back to me and said "Not anymore he isn't. As of right now, he is no one's slave ANYMORE!" I'm sure the look on my face told her that I was not playing but when I extended my extra pistol to Moses, she knew then that I was serious. He slowly reached for the gun looking at Hannah as if he needed her approval. "Go on and take it. Have you ever used one of these before?" I asked him. The moment his hand touched the handle his eyes lit up like a child with a new Christmas toy. He stroked the barrel of the gun and nodded his head yes. "Now put that in your coat pocket or something. It only needs to come out if you need to use it. You understand?" I said. Moses nodded his head again but with a huge smile. I knew then that I had gained not only his trust but his loyalty. I was going to need it for us to be successful when we got to the plantation. "Let's eat! I'm hungry." I told the two.

We walked inside with Hannah in front. The moment we entered all eyes were on us. The saloon was packed with all kinds of people from the well off to the bottom of the barrel. The music from the stage show traveled throughout the saloon and the chatter from the crowd was just as loud. We weaved our way through the smoke filled crowd that was surrounding the bar. Most of the tables were taken but we found one against a wall in the back left corner of the place. A high stakes card game was going on at the table to our right. In front of us was another table with two men being entertained by one of the bar maids. She was fanning her ruffled dress and showing as much thigh as she could without exposing her lady parts. She rolled and bounced from one man to the next until a familiar face caught her attention. It was none other than Bella herself. Bella stood a few feet away from the table behind the men's backs. They realized that someone had their entertainer's attention when she sat up and stop frolicking all over them. Like a child caught by her parent in the act of being promiscuous the bar maid jumped to her feet and dashed away past Bella in a fast walking pace. The two fellows turned to see where she was scurrying off to and met Bella's glaring smirk. From the looks of her deceptively beautiful sweet smile, you never would have known that she was as cunning as any outlaw east of the Mississippi River. The two men figured that out when they went to stand and Bella motioned for them to have a seat. It wasn't her good looks or mischief grin that convinced them to do so. It was the two shot derringer she held concealed in the palm of her hand visible only to the two of them. Without hesitation they slowly but surely took their seats as suggested. Once they were seated she slowly turned and walked off in the direction of where the barmaid ran off. The men were clearly frustrated but not enough to take a hot one. They waved her off and turned their attention to the stage show. I couldn't help for wondering what Bella was going to do next. I saw the barmaid run outside so I knew Bella was going to follow her. Hannah and Moses were none the wiser about what just happened and didn't need to be. I stood to follow Bella and Hannah grabbed my hand. "Where are you going?" she asked. Both she and

Moses looked confused. "Relax, I'm just going to get some fresh air. All of this smoke is burning my eyes. I won't be long." I assured them. "But what about some food? Ain't you hungry?" Moses asked looking even more concerned than Hannah. "Of course I am. Just have them to bring me whatever you get." I said then patted him on the back and rushed outside before Bella got too far away. I made it outside just in time to see Bella kick off her shoes and grab up the front of her dress then take off running down the side of the saloon. I'd never seen a woman run so fast in a dress and if I hadn't taken off behind her when I did, I still wouldn't have because in a flash she was gone like the wind. She was so focused on catching the retreating barmaid so badly that she never noticed me behind her. The two of them slipped behind the saloon to a dead end. I stopped just short of turning the corner so that I could spy on what was going on without being seen by either. I could hear the barmaid begging Bella "Please Bella. You don't have to do this. I swear it won't happen again. I promise!" Slowly Bella walked up to the woman closing in on her one slow step at a time. Stupidly the woman reached in her brassiere and pulled out barber's razor. She raised it high in the air and shouted "That's enough! Don't make me have to cut you Bella. If you come near me I swear I will kill you in this alley tonight." Bella stopped and stood still. She tilted her head to the right then to the left and began to walk towards the woman again. "Did you hear me BITCH? I said don't move!" the barmaid screamed. Her face turned beet red as her eyes bucked in disbelief that Bella was not obeying her commands. "Do you want to die? Why are you still coming?" Bella stopped and said "Because my name ain't bitch...BITCH!" That's when the barmaid gathered enough heart to charge Bella but was thrown back by the blast from Bella's derringer. The woman fell to the ground on her back. Bella walked up to her and squatted over the gasping woman. She placed the barrel of her smoking hot pistol directly into the bullet hole in the woman's chest so that she could feel the hot metal in her wound. She stood to her feet and said "You should have known better than to bring a knife to a gun fight. Now who's the bitch?" Then she put the woman out of her misery with the other bullet to the head.

She turned to walk away from the dead woman then stopped in her tracks when she noticed me leaning against the building with my feet and arms crossed. She put her pistol away in her small purse then adjusted her clothes and started to walk towards me. I had seen enough so I turned and began walking back to rejoin Moses and Hannah in the saloon. I could hear her yelling out "Hey you. Hey I know that you hear me." I in fact did hear her but kept walking. By the time she caught up with me I was entering the saloon doors. Just as I was walking through the doors I felt a tug at my left arm. I turned to face her but it wasn't Bella. It was Hannah and she was crying hysterically. I couldn't make out a word she was saying other than "…they're going to kill him. Hurry!" it wasn't until she pointed in the direction of where we were sitting that I understood what she was trying to tell me. When I looked over I saw that Moses was surrounded by the two fellows the dead barmaid was entertaining. I pushed my way through the crowd until I made it close enough to place the barrel of my gun to the back of the head of one of the men. "Now this doesn't look like a fair fight gentlemen. What seems to be the problem here?" I said to them. I removed the pistol from the holster of the guy I had my gun on. He slowly raised his hands to surrender. His buddy stood to the left of him and whipped around to see who I was. His eyes grew bigger than apples when he saw my gun pointed at his buddy's head. He turned to face me head on and said "You niggers don't know who you're fucking with do you?" I chuckled and responded "And I really don't give a fuck. Now slowly hand over your gun or I'll blow a hole in the back of his head quicker than a cat can lick his ass." He held his hand up and said "Now just take it easy. No need to do anything crazy here. Just hold on one minute. Your friend here insulted my brother when all he did was try to tell the lady that the owner didn't like slaves in his establishment. Then he got all huffy talking about he wasn't a slave. We just wanted to see his papers if he was truly free. That's all. I swear." I giggled and asked Moses "Is that true big man? You told him that you weren't a slave?" Moses was sweating like a guilty man on trial. He bucked his eyes and said "That's what you told me Cody. You says I'm not a slave no more. That's what you says to me. And I'm not. So that's what I told him."

124

Moses was so nervous that he was trembling like a leaf in the wind when he nodded yes. "You did right big man. You're not a slave." I reassured him. The next thing I heard was a loud grunt from the guy standing next to me. His eyes and mouth shot wide open. Then from behind him I heard a woman's voice say "You didn't get his gun. He was reaching for it to blow YOUR head off." The voice was Bella's. She peeked from behind the man's back and said "Now let's get the hell out of here. We're going to have to take them with us. So lower your pistol to his lower back so that no one sees you escorting this white man out by gun point. Now we're all going to walk out of here like old friends taking the party somewhere else. We don't have much more time before this bastard drops dead on us and then we're all fucked. So you two good white boys are going to grin and bear it all the way through the saloon doors as if we were one big fucked up family. Moses you get right behind me and good looking you bring your man right behind him. Now let's go gentlemen." She stepped to the side of her guy and put her arm around his back then had him to put his arm around her shoulder. She led him and the rest of us straight out of the saloon just as she said we would. When we got outside I realized what she did to the guy. When he reached for his gun hidden in the back of his pants she stabbed him in the hand with a huge knife. The knife went completely through the palm of his hand and into his back. It was pinning his hand to his back so that he couldn't move it. We walked across the street and slid behind the bank where no one could see us. Bella pointed them in the direction of the town's doctor to have the blade removed before the guy passed out and died.

Chapter 11

Every Rose Has A Thorn

After everything that went on that night
Hannah was nowhere to be found. Bella went back
to the inn to check for her because she said Moses
and I would probably run into some trouble if we
went back without Hannah. She was right. Had we
shown up alone there would have been questions
that we couldn't have answered and would have
ended up hanging dead from a tree somewhere.
She was familiar around those parts so it was less
attention if she entered alone. Once she determined
that Hannah had abandoned us she took us back to
her place for the night. She lived in a small one
bedroom shack hidden in the middle of nowhere
surrounded by large trees. It was deep off of the
beaten path, secluded far away from town. We had
to steal three horses from the saloon in order to get
there. It was old and in need of much work but it

was far better than the hut I left behind. It was as though she transformed into a completely different person once we got to her home. She was the perfect lady. She allowed us to stay and even cooked for us. When we were done eating Moses passed out sleep on the floor. I decided to step outside for a smoke and to clear my head. The night air was refreshing and still. The stars were scattered across the sky and surrounded the crescent moon. There were two old rocking chairs sitting on the porch next to one another that looked like they had been unbothered for years. I took a seat in one then pulled out a cigarette and match stick. I was halfway through with my smoke when I heard the door open and footsteps on the porch. It was Bella. She had changed into her nightgown and gotten relaxed for the evening. She took a seat in the other chair next to me. "What kind of tobacco is that you're smoking? It smells funny." she asked. "It's not tobacco. It's hemp. It grows wild near my old home." I explained. She leaned back in her seat then stared out into the trees and said "You know, there's something mysterious about you. I like it. You're not like most of the black men I've ever met. You're definitely not a slave trying to pretend to be a free man because you speak too well." She looked over her shoulder in the direction of the house and said "Now that poor big son of a bitch in there curled up on my floor, he's a slave. I can see who and what he was from a mile away. But not you, you're different. What's your story? And pass that funny smelling cigarette over here and let me try it because it's different like you. And I like trying different things. What's your name handsome?" I passed her my cigarette and gave her what she wanted. I told her everything about me from my childhood on up to that very moment. I even told her about Sleeping Flower and the baby. It had been years since I'd had someone to talk to that way. It felt good to be able to talk about some of the things that kept me up many sleepless nights afraid to close my eyes for fear of images of my family being gunned down in front of me. She allowed me to get it all out and it felt great.

"Now that you know everything about me it's your turn. What is YOUR story?" I inquired in exchange. She stood and walked to the edge of the porch and placed both hands on the porch rail. She lowered her head and glanced over her left shoulder at me then said in a soft voice "What do you want to know?" Right away I knew that she had quite the story to tell of herself. Slowly she turned to face me head on. "I want to know who is the woman they call Bella Rose." I said. She lowered her head and asked "How do you know my name?" I answered, "Hannah told me. She said that you were trouble and to stay away from you. But like you, I like people and things that are different." She smiled at me and I swear my heart stopped beating for a moment. The moon casted the perfect backlight creating a silhouette underneath her gown with more curves than side winding rattlesnake. Her breast set high and full. Her hips were perfectly shaped like a pear. Her thick curly black hair was cut short and round like a ball. Her dimples were what I would imagine a sea of warm caramel would look. Her plump lips had me in a trance as I clung to her every word. "So is that why you followed me outside? You wanted to see if what the white girl said was true? So what do you think? Do you think I'm trouble too?" she questioned. I sat back in my chair and crossed my legs then said "I think that I need to hear your side before I think anything." "Good answer." she said. She sat back down in her seat and said "First off, the woman from the alley was strictly business. The old man that you saw me with hired me to take care of her. You see I do debt collections among other things to make a living. And some people don't understand that because they have been privileged all of their lives. Like that white girl Hannah, I know who she is. Unlike hers, my mother was born a slave. So I too was born a slave. But like her father, my father was also born a white man. When I was a child I grew up not knowing who my father was until his wife found out. She learned that her husband Theodore Benjamin Frost, the heir to Frost Enterprise fathered a nigger baby. She had given him four boys that all grew to become prominent figures in town. But I was the daughter he longed for that his wife couldn't seem to provide. He secretly taught me many things that the other slaves were forbidden to learn. By the time I was nine I could read and write as well as any adult white man or woman. I often wondered why I was allowed to sleep in the big house while even my mother was forced to stay in the slave quarters. I eventually learned that it was because the misses wouldn't allow any of the female slaves that she thought were pretty to come inside of the big house for any reason. She knew of her husband's obsession with the female slaves, especially the pretty and shapely ones like my mother. But while she was patrolling the inside of her home she should have been checking the woodshed late at night. That's where he forced himself on whoever he chose while his wife slept. My mother was apparently his favorite which didn't sit too well with one jealous ass house nigger in particular named Nephi. She was a maid that lived in the big house unlike my mother. It was no secret among the slaves that she was sweet on master. He even knew it but refused to give her the time of day. It all came to a head when my mother was told to deliver word to master that one of the field hands had passed out. When my mother got to the house Nephi refused to allow her to relay the message. Because of that the field hand died and that meant it was going to cost master money. When master questioned my mother why she didn't do as she was told and deliver the news, my mother told him everything. This of course angered master. He had Nephi whipped for her disobedience. As you could imagine, this made Nephi hate my mother even more. The first chance she got Nephi high tailed it straight to the misses and told her all about my mother and me. Needless to say the misses was not pleased. She was so upset that she ordered my mother to be tied to a wagon wheel and whipped. I and the rest of the slaves were forced to watch the overseer whip my mother until there was no life left in her body. My mother's body was ripped to shreds as we all watched. No matter how much I screamed and begged for him to stop the more the misses demanded he continued. Even after my mother's lifeless body laid slumped over the bloody wagon wheel the misses showed no mercy and ordered him to continue. Pieces of her flesh began to tear away from his thrashing. Had master not rode up on his horse and seen what was going on she probably would still be getting whipped. He had been gone away in town most of the day and had no idea what was happening. He immediately ordered the overseer to stop and demanded that I be released from the grips of another cracker that was holding me back. We both rushed over to my mother's side. The blood dripped from both my mother and the wheel. Master untied her hands then sat on the ground holding and rocking her limp body. Patches of her hair and scalp had been ripped away from her body by the whip. All I could do was stand there looking at him holding her and crying my eyes out. I kept thinking that the way he held her made me feel like he may have even loved my mother. But if that was the case then how could he allow her to live and die that way? I haven't cried a tear since that day. Two days later I was sold off and sent away to another plantation. I was there three days before I ran. Three times I ran and three times they caught me. Then it was off to the next plantation. Home of Preston J. Maxwell and Alice Maxwell. There I was forced to work in the house for the exact opposite reason why the Frosts' didn't allow my mother and others like her inside of their house. Master Maxwell was like my father. He couldn't keep his hands off of the female slaves either. He was a lot older but had the sexual appetite of a twenty year old. Many nights several of us were forced to please him and each other for his entertainment. He was a filthy pig of a man. His teenage son was no better. His son Walter thought the world off me. He would have me to come see him quite often without his father's knowledge. His obsession with me eventually led to my opportunity to be free, free of both of them and the life of a slave. One night I convinced him that he and I could be together just the two of us but only if his parents were no longer in the picture. Together we torched the plantation while his parents slept. Once we knew that they could not escape the flames in the house I put a bullet in his head and ran until the name Frost was no longer important. From Alabama to Maryland I did whatever it took to survive even if that meant robbing or killing. But I will DIE before I live another day as a slave!" Bella's body was trembling and filled with hate from having relived some of the horrible things that she had been through. Right then I made up my mind that I would do any and everything in my power to make sure that she'd never have to experience that life ever again.

After sharing our unique stories we both agreed that we should get some much needed rest. Now that Hannah was nowhere to be found we needed a new plan because I was not going back to my hut. That night I slept on the old dusty couch

Bella had in the main room while she slept in her bed and Moses stayed on the floor. In the morning I got up to find Bella and an old white guy sitting at her table talking. I rubbed the sleep out of my eyes to make sure I was seeing what I thought I was seeing. Not only was it a white guy, it was the old white man that she was with in the inn. When Bella heard me sitting up she turned around in her seat and said "I see you finally decided to join us. Good morning. This is Mr. Ronald Langford. Mr. Langford is going to help us get onto the plantation by pretending to be a traveling jewelry salesman. A woman like Hannah's mother can't resist an opportunity to purchase a piece of fine jewelry. Chances are Hannah's hauled ass back home by now. There's no telling how she's going to explain why she came back home alone. So we can't just rush up in there just to get shot dead. Cody, you and Moses can stay here with me for the next few days until we strike out." Moses was beginning to wake up from his sleep as well. Bella pointed at Moses and told me "I have a couple of six shooters and plenty of shells. Do you think you can teach him how to shoot a pistol in the next couple of days? We may need an extra gun." I looked over at the confusion on Moses' face and knew that I had my work cut out for me but I replied "Don't worry he will be ready." Bella smiled and said "Good. I like a man with confidence. It's sexy." All that I could do was smile. Mr. Langford broke the awkward silence with "Meanwhile I need to head back to town and find some jewelry to present to this woman. Bella I will be back in a couple of days." He stood and walked to the door then turned and said "Make sure they are ready." He left and Bella went to her room then shut the door. When she came out she had her purse and hat. "Where are you going?" I asked. "I have a few things that I need to take care of in town. I will be back around nightfall. If you get hungry help yourselves to whatever is in here. I will bring dinner from the saloon when I come back." She reached in her purse and pulled out two pistols then handed them to me. "There are bullets in a large wooden box in the kitchen cabinet. Just look and you'll find them." she advised. Then I watched her twist her perfectly shaped hips across the room and out of the door.

Chapter 12

The Reconstruction of A Man

Moses and I wasted no time getting target practice in for him. We setup a few targets behind the house for him to shoot. Surprisingly enough he wasn't too bad for someone that had never had shooting lessons before. I was really impressed at just how quickly he was learning. When we finished he and I went inside to have some lunch and wait for Bella to return. The sun was setting and I was beginning to get a little worried about Bella. I walked out onto the porch and took a seat in the same rocking chair from the night before. It wasn't long before Moses joined me. He took the seat next to me and said "You really like this woman huh?" The smile on my face obviously answered his question. "Oh yeah, you reeealy like her. I can tell by the way your eyes light up when you talk to her and the way you hang on to her every word. I can't say that I blame you. She's very pretty. You remind me of the way my Maye makes me feel" Moses told me as he stared out into the open field with a big smile on his face. It was apparent that he missed the love of his life. Then he lowered his head and said "I hate to think about what might be happening to her with Hannah going back without me. If that damn Jacob lays a hand on her I will…" Before he could even finish his sentence I interrupted him "Hey don't even think like that. She's going to be fine when we get there. I know it's easy for me to say but you have to stay focused if we're going to get your family out of there." He nodded his head and wiped away a tear from his eye. He stood up and said "I think I will go in and get a little sleep." He started to head back inside then stopped and said "Thanks for everything Cody. This is the first time in my life that I've ever felt free. I want my family to know this feeling." Then he walked back inside leaving me speechless. I had been blessed to not know the feeling of being enslaved as he and Bella once lived. He made me appreciate my life of freedom even more. We all had a rough life but at that moment I felt sorry for them both.

After awhile the sun slowly set behind the tree line. The evening came in with me fast asleep on the porch glued to the rocking chair. The cool breeze was so relaxing that I could have slept there until morning. The sound of a horse trotting interrupted my not so deep sleep. It was Bella returning from town on a new horse none the less. She walked onto the porch carrying a large bag and a smaller bag. "What's in the bags?" I asked still half asleep. "Some things for you and Moses. Wipe the drool off of your face and come inside." she advised with a laugh at my messy mouth. I followed her into the house where Moses was still asleep in his same spot in a corner on the floor. She walked into the kitchen and sat the smaller bag on the kitchen table and tossed the larger bag to me. "When was the last time you had a bath?" she asked in a lower voice to keep from waking Moses. "It's been awhile. I could sure use one." I answered. "There are a couple of buckets out back by the well. If you bring some water in I will heat it up for you to bathe. Then you can try on the clothes I got for you in the bag. I brought back some bread and things to make a soup. I'll start on that while you get the water. We'll let ole Moses keep resting. When he gets up he can bathe and try on his clothes as well." she suggested as she continued to pull things from her food back. "Why are you still standing there? I thought you wanted to wash your ass." she said with a smile. "Go on and get now. It's going to take me awhile to heat up that water unless you want to take a cold bath." she continued when she saw me chuckling at her. I headed out of the door to do my water run and heard Bella mumble under her breath "That's what I thought. You don't want your nuts to freeze." Before I went completely out I responded "I heard that." And without missing a beat she said "It was meant for you to hear." I knew right then that it was best that I kept my mouth shut and continue out of the door.

We enjoyed our meal and I allowed Moses to bathe first since he had gone the longest without one and smelled the strongest. Bella and I sat on the porch enjoying the cool breeze while Moses freshened up. She shared a bottle of whiskey with me and I shared another of my cigarettes with her. We also shared more stories of our pasts with each other. Before long we had drank half of her bottle and smoke two cigarettes. We laughed and poked fun at some of the things that we thought were strange about white folks and some of the things they did. After drinking and laughing for so long nature called and I had to relieve myself. I stood from my rocking chair and said "Now I don't know if I can make it all the way to the outhouse before I piss on myself. You'll have to excuse me for pissing on the side of the house but I really need to drain the dragon." I stepped down off of the porch and headed around to the side of the house to handle my business. Before I disappeared around the corner I heard Bella utter "A dragon huh? We'll see." I staggered on around to the side of the house and dared not make the same mistake as earlier and let on that I heard what she said. I knew that she was aware of me knowing. When I returned Bella was in the house already. When I walked in Moses was sitting in a chair at the kitchen table trying on a new shirt. He stood to his feet to adjust the garment. Although the shirt fit him perfectly, I believe the fact that he had never had anything new is what brought a tear to his eye. He stood in the middle of the floor with his arms stretched out in front of himself admiring his new gift from Bella. It was a drastically noticeable improvement from the dirt filled shirt he had been wearing for God knows how many years. "Look…look at what Bella got for me Cody. For ME! She said it's for me to HAVE." he told me with tears in his eyes and voice. It only got worse when Bella returned from her bedroom with a pair of trousers for him to try on as well. That's when the large man dropped to his knees and began to cry uncontrollably. Bella walked over to console him. He wrapped his arms around her legs and cried even harder. She stroked his head as he tried his best to thank her but his tears kept getting in the way. "Shhhhh. You don't have to thank me. We are in this world together to help one another. You are my brother and I…I am your sister." she whispered softly to him. "Now try on the britches and let me see how they fit." she advised Moses. Slowly he gathered himself and took the pants to Bella's room to change. That entire exchange was sobering. I was damn near moved to tears myself but I maintained my composure.

"That was amazingly generous of you." I told Bella. She looked over at me and said "Well thank you. I have some things for you to try on also once you have bathed." I was flattered but unmoved by her generosity. Unlike Moses, I was no slave and didn't dress as one so I saw no need for new clothes. I often cleaned my clothes in the river and were not nearly as worn thin as Moses' clothes. My pants were made from the youngest animal hides for long lasting durability. I was almost offended at the implication that I was in need. "Thank you but I don't need new clothes. The ones I'm wearing may need to be washed but there's no need to replace them." I suggested. She giggled and said "Suit yourself. If you want to keep walking around looking like a black Indian then that's fine by me. But if you don't want to stick out of a crowd like a sore thumb then I suggest you reconsider. Besides, I think that you would look a lot more handsome and a lot more civilized in the right clothing." She walked over to me then softly caressed the side of my face and added "Not to mention, no woman is going to want to be with a man wearing dead animal skins around his tail every day." She leaned in to give me a kiss and I leaned in to meet her until we were interrupted by Moses coming out of the room yelling "They fit! Look Cody, I'm is a new man! Maybe she has something for you too." His eyes and smile were both wider than the river. He ran over and grabbed Bella up off of her feet and started spinning her around saying "thank you" over and over before finally putting her down. His excitement was contagious. "While you two were on the porch I emptied the tub then refilled it with warm water. You should go wash and see what she has for you. I know if she got something for me then she definitely got something for you." Moses suggested. Bella smiled with a wicked grin and looked over at me then said "I sure do." A woman with eyes and a smile like Bella's could make any man fold. "Ok…ok. I'll go get cleaned up and see what you have for me." I advised them both then headed to the bedroom where the tub was located. I closed the bedroom door behind me but could still hear the two of them laughing and having fun with Moses' new digs.

I got undressed and into the tub of warm water. It had been years since I had been in an actual tub. The last one was when I was a child back in my old home in New York. I sat there enjoying the nostalgic feeling of being younger and back in New York before my life was suddenly turned upside down. The memories of my family and days of old filled my head and began to take over my emotions. I was only moments away from possibly breaking down in tears when the door slowly opened. That's when Bella entered the room. Quickly I covered my balls with my hands. I was so deep into my thoughts that I didn't realize the laughing and talking in the main part of the house had stopped. She walked over and stood in front of the tub with her hands on her hips. She looked down into the tub and said "Trust me you don't have anything down there that I've never seen before. So relax and bathe before the water turns ice cold and turn that dragon into a yard lizard. Besides, you have big hands but they're not big enough to cover all of that." Then she walked off and left me there chuckling at myself. She tossed a wash rag over my shoulder and into the tub for me to use. Next was a large hand sized chunk of homemade soap that followed with a splash. I took Bella's advice and began to bathe quickly before the water did in fact cool off and leave me looking about as hung as a little boy. I was nearly finished with the exception of my lower legs and feet when I turned around to say "Thank you." to Bella. When I turned around she was pulling a chair up to the tub. She sat in the chair with my head between her knees. She leaned my head back and reached into the water. She grabbed the hunk of soap and lathered my beard then pulled out a razor. I was speechless. She shaved my face cleaner than it had been in years. The gentle touch of her hand made my Johnson rise out of the water. "Looks like your dragon is peeking out of the water." she said with a little laugh. She stood up and slid the chair away from the tub then walked off. I sat there for a minute rubbing my smooth face then turned again to say "Thank you." but I never got to say it because when I looked up my eyes and mind were filled with beauty. Bella was standing there with her back to me and as naked as the day she was born. The light from the flickering flame of the oil lamps in the room danced around her beautiful golden skin. After getting an eye full for a moment, I cleared my throat as loudly as possible to get her attention. It worked and when she turned around Bella displayed a perfect pair of breasts that sat up nice and high. Her flat stomach and slim waist led down to her hour glass shaped hips that had my jaw hanging. She walked over to the tub and stuck a foot inside. Before she could get the other one in I asked "Do you want me to get out?" She paused and said "That's on you. Do you want to get out?" I was like a speechless child. All I could do was shake my head no. She didn't waste any time joining me.

She took a seat in the water between my legs with her back to me. She got as close to me as possible and leaned against my chest. She lathered her breast with soap then held her head back and slowly raised her wash rag above her head. Water ran from the rag rinsing the soap away. I couldn't resist running my hands across her glistening skin. Although I was aiding the removal of the soap I took much pleasure in feeling her slick breast and erect nipples in my hands. It was no secret that she enjoyed it as well. "It's been years since I've been touched this gently." she confessed. She laid her head back on my shoulder then closed her eyes. Our lips were drawn together like magnets. The mere touch of her lips sent tingles down my back that not even Sleeping Flower had made me feel. She raised her bottom out of the water just enough to gradually come back down on my manhood.

The sounds of her moans of pleasure excited me to no end. She leaned forward and pulled me along with her until she was on her knees gripping the sides of the tub with me still deep inside of her love. Over and over we loved on each other splashing water over the top of the tub. I feared that her screams would awaken Moses but she didn't seem to care at all. The floor was soaked with bath water from our bodies clashing together rapidly. We forced water from the tub and from both of us at the same time. Exhausted and drained we both collapsed over the side of the tub with Bella underneath my well loved body. I knew right then that it was at that moment we fell in love with one another. We spent the rest of the night making love to each other. Bella did things to me with her mouth that Sleeping Flower had never done or probably didn't know how. It was apparent that she was no stranger to sex but had some pinned up animalistic desires that hadn't been met in quite some time. I met every one of her desires and introduced her to some of mine as well. I took advantage of my opportunity to make a good first sexual impression. I made sure that I pleased her every need before allowing her or myself to sleep for the night. Her deep sleep and loud snoring confirmed that not only had I done my job but that it was a job well done.

Chapter 13

Time To Show and Prove

That next morning we were awakened by the large fist of Moses pounding on the bedroom door. He was on the other side of the door yelling "Get up! We have company riding up." Bella and I jumped out of bed and to our feet still naked from the night before. She hurried and put on a robe and tossed me the bag of clothes she brought back.

"Here get dressed. I hope you can wear everything." she said then rushed out of the room to see who was coming. I emptied the bag onto the bed and rushed to get dressed. Luckily everything fit perfectly even the black leather vest. It was as though she had me with her when she got the things. I felt like Moses when he tried on his new clothes but I didn't have time to admire myself. I had to hurry to see what was going on outside. I walked out to join Bella and Moses on the porch. I was strapping my gun belt on when I walked through the front door. I adjusted my new black hat and stood in the doorway looking out at the man riding up on his horse. It was the older guy from the inn. He rode up to the house and hopped off of his horse with a saddlebag in his hand. He walked onto the porch and gave Bella a peck on the cheek. He took a couple of looks at Moses and I then said "Well you two look a sight better than the last time I saw you." then he walked past Bella and Moses to get to the doorway where I was standing. He looked me up and down and said "And you sir clean up exceptionally well. Now if you will excuse me, I'd like to enter so that we can get to work." I stepped aside to let him inside. He had a funny accent and waddled a little when he walked. He took a seat at the kitchen table and plopped the saddlebag down on the table. He turned his attention back to the three of us and said "Well don't just stand there. Come on, I have some things to show you." Bella was the first to start heading back inside. Before she walked in she stop where I was standing and said in a sultry voice "Damn! He's right. You look great. Almost as good as you tasted." She walked on in and Moses followed behind her but not without giving me a wink and two thumbs up. I walked in behind them and shaking my head with a chuckle.

The four of us took a seat at the table while Mr. Langford dumped his saddlebag onto the table.

It was full of all kinds of jewels and jewelry. He spread out the large pile and said "This should be enough to convince Scarlett and the others that I am a jewel dealer. Once I get inside of the house with her, chances are Jacob and the others will not be interested in hanging around. That's when I can force her to show me where the money is hidden. You three will have to do the rest." Bella turned to Moses and asked "Is there a way to sneak onto the plantation without being seen?" Moses thought for half of a second then said "There are many trails through the woods. One of them takes you to the backside of the house that not many people know about. We call it the dark trail because only the slaves use it to steal away at night when they want to have a little privacy. It takes you to a really high mountain side. It's hard to climb and many slaves have fallen to their deaths trying to escape. We would have to go along the edge of the woods and walk around until we got to the backside of the house but we can get on there." At that moment I realized we still needed more help or else we were going to be in big trouble. "Moses do you think that you could get some of others to help overtake the place?" I asked. "Hell yeah. Whatever you need Cody." he answered. I stood to my feet and started pacing back and forth to get my thoughts together. "The others don't really need to be marksmen. The sight of slaves with guns should be enough. But we will need more guns for the others." Bella stood then walked up to me and said "And I know just where to get them. A place that has more guns and shells than we can carry." Mr. Langford's head snapped up from fiddling with his jewels. "You're not thinking of doing what I think you are thinking of doing...are you?" he asked of Bella with a smirk on his face. "You bet your snow white ass I am. But we'll have to get them tonight while most of the town is attending the mayor's ball. All of the sheriffs and elected officials will be too busy kissing each others' asses to even notice before it's too late. We'll be in and out then back here in no time. This is perfect." Bella exclaimed. "You've wanted to hit that place for quite some time now. It looks like you have a reason and a team to help pull it off." Mr. Langford added. Moses slowly raised his hand like a child in school and said "Umm excuse me but what is we talking about now?" The look on his face was so innocent and childlike that it brought laughter and smiles to the three of us. To help him get up to speed I told him "She's talking about robbing the gun store back in town. All of the lawmen and important white folks will be at a party for the mayor it sounds like. So it should be pretty easy without anyone noticing." The look and sigh of relief from Moses brought on even more laughter. It was all cut short when Mr. Langford's laughter turned into uncontrollable coughing and gagging. A look of concern fell on all of our faces. He retrieved a handkerchief from his inside coat pocket to cover his mouth while he attempted to gather himself. "Are you ok Ron?" Bella asked with a look of terror in her eyes. "I'm fine. I just got a little choked up. I'm not a young man anymore you know? Too much excitement can trigger things in this old body of mine." he answered. "Sit tight, I'll get you some water." Bella offered before bolting out of the door to the well outside.

Mr. Langford spent the day with me and Moses while Bella went into town to scope out the gun shop before we did the job. I gave Moses more shooting lessons while Mr. Langford napped on the couch. He was awakening when Moses and I were coming in from target practice. "So have you gotten any better at it?" Mr. Langford asked in a half sleep raspy voice. Moses sat his pistol on the table and said with a huge smile on his face "I'm better today than I was yesterday." Mr. Langford looked up at Moses and said "I was actually talking to Cody." His words froze me in my tracks. I looked over at him and said "My shooting is fine. I don't need to practice." I started to take my gun belt off and he stopped me by saying "Horse shit!" Again I was frozen by his words. "Excuse me I asked." trying not to lose my temper. He was Bella's friend, not mine. I didn't want to disrespect the old guy so again I said "Excuse me." He sat up on the couch and put his feet on the floor then said "Everyone needs practice. Unless you're Jesus Christ son, you're not perfect." He stood up then stretched and yawned loudly with a roaring grunt. He scratched his crotch then headed out of the back door saying "Grab some more shells and come with me." On his way out he grabbed the pistol that Moses was using. I did as he asked and grabbed more shells then met him and Moses outside. I gave him a handful of bullets for him to load his pistol. "Moses if you don't mind, could you go over there and get one of the cans you have setup for practice? Thank you kindly sir." he requested. Without hesitation Moses jumped to it. He grabbed one of the cans and began to walk back with it when Mr. Langford stopped him. "No…no stay there with it. When I tell you to, I want you to toss the can high in the air." he asked. He then looked at me and said "Anyone can hit a still target. But can you hit a moving object?" He turned back to Moses and yelled "Now!" On command Moses tossed the can high into the sky as commanded. When the can reached the peak of its flight Mr. Langford raised the pistol from his side and let off two shots hitting the can twice before it fell to the ground. I was impressed so I gave him a slow clap for his performance. I looked Mr. Langford in the eyes and said "Moses throw it up again please." Again as requested, Moses bent over, grabbed the can and tossed it in the air again. I turned and drew my pistol then emptied all six bullets into the falling can. As the can was coming down I whipped out my hunting knife and threw it. The large blade pierced the can through both sides and stuck deep into a nearby tree with the can pinned to the tree. Again I looked the old man in his eyes then said "I'm not Jesus but this is what I do Mr. Langford. Like I said, my shooting skills are fine." I walked off leaving the two of them in disbelief. I was impressed by Mr. Langford but not moved.

The old man came inside not long after I did leaving Moses outside alone. He took a bottle of liquor and two glasses out of the kitchen cabinets then had a seat at the kitchen table with me. He poured a shot for me and a double for himself. He drank his glassful before I could even pick my glass up then poured himself another double. "So tell me Cody, what do you plan to do with your share of the money when this is all said and done?" he asked. "Well Mr. Langford I plan to get a home and maybe have enough land to do some farming.

If I'm lucky maybe I can find a woman to settle down with one day and have kids. What about you? What do you plan to do with your cut?" I asked. He chuckled a bit then said "Me? Oh I'm not taking a cut. This job is for the three of you. I have no need for more money. I already have more than I will spend before my days are up. I'm just in it to help you three…and for the pure thrill. However, I do have a rather generous proposition for you if you're interested in truly following through with your plans you just told me about." At that moment he had my full attention and I was all ears. "Oh yeah, what is it?" I asked. He then knocked down the remainder of his second drink and slammed the glass down on the table. He poured himself a third glass while my first remained untouched. Then he said "Well you see…I'm dying Cody. I don't have the heart to tell Bella and I would prefer that you respect my wish to keep this a secret from her and Moses. Bella told me your story and I think that you would be the perfect person to turn my estate over to. I have an unoccupied plantation sitting on over two hundred acres of land sitting on the Maryland and Virginia state line. I never owned slaves nor did I ever agree with it. So you can take that look off of your face and relax. I inherited it from my father's sister, my aunt Clara. Now she and her husband did in fact own over a hundred slaves before my uncle passed away. It wasn't long before Aunt Clara realized that she was nowhere nearly as business savvy as my uncle. Well to make a long story short, she eventually lost everything accept for the house. A few months after hitting rock bottom her health began to fail her. The doctor said she died from pneumonia but I think she died from grieving over her husband. They didn't have any children of their own so she chose me to leave the place in her will but I'm not sure why. She had other nieces and nephews that she could have left it with other than me. I hated going to visit because of the way they treated their slaves. But none the less she left it to me anyways. It's been well over ten years since anyone has lived in the place. I'm willing to sell it to you for a little of nothing once you get your cut…that is if you are interested. I'm sure it's going to need some repairs after being left unattended for so long. It's out in the middle of nowhere and you can live in peace. The closest sign of civilization is over sixty miles away. Who knows, maybe you can even talk Bella into making it a home together." That's when I took my drink down after hearing about this opportunity to start a new life. He stood with his drink in hand then headed for the couch. "So what's the catch?" I asked. He took a seat on the couch and in one gulp he finished his third drink. He sat his empty glass on the floor then laid back and said "You have to allow me to stay there free of charge until I check out of this thing called life. I'm going to take a nap while you think about it. Wake me when Bella gets back. You can also give me your decision when I wake up" He closed his eyes and was asleep in no time. As quick as he went to sleep I had made up my mind to accept his offer just as quickly.

Chapter 14
Game Time

When Bella finally arrived back to the house both Moses and Mr. Langford were still fast asleep. I met her on the porch before she came inside and disturbed the two of them. I wanted a chance to speak to her alone about Mr. Langford's offer. "Hello there handsome. How was your day?" she asked walking onto the porch. I walked up to her and placed my hands around her waist then said "It's been really interesting but now that you're back it's gotten even better." She gave me a peck on the lips then handed me a bag she was carrying. "I swear you come back with a bag of something every time you leave woman. What is this?" I jokingly asked. She smiled and sashayed over to her rocking chair. "I got a little something for Moses. Take a look." she suggested while taking a seat. I reached inside and found two brand new Colt pistols and a gun belt. "They're for Moses. Every man needs his own guns. It's time he has his." she said with a smile of accomplishment. She was right. If he was to ever be free then he would need to feel free and nothing gave a man the sense of freedom like a pair of pistols. I realized then that Bella was even more special than I imagined. I saw a side of compassion that only women have. It let me know that even with all of the pain and anger she deals with daily that deep down she has a loving soul. "Wow! That was both deep and true." I said and took a seat next to her. "Tell me, how do you know Mr.

Langford?" I asked. She smiled then sat back in her chair and said "I met him not long after I escaped from the Frost Plantation. I was living in anywhere that I could find from town to town, eating whatever I could find. Until one day I got caught stealing food from the garbage behind a saloon in Williamsburg, Virginia. Ron convinced the owner that I was his slave and was ordered to stay outside behind the saloon. He promised the owner that he would deal with me and that it would never happen again. The owner let me leave with Ron and never said a word to the sheriff. After that Ron offered to bring me further north to a safer life. I thought that he was going to turn out to be like all of the other white men that I had come across. I thought that he was only saving me from one hell just to put me in another. I thought that he was just looking to have his way with me. I was preparing to send him to his maker if he tried. Turned out that I was completely wrong about him. In exchange for his generosity all he asked was that I help him with little odds and in jobs here and there. As a matter of fact this house was once his. He wanted to give it to me but wouldn't accept it for free. I paid him by doing some of the jobs and putting my pay towards paying off the cost of the house. In a way he's been the closest thing to a father that I've ever had. I owe my life to him." Her words were a bit shocking. I was not expecting her to be so affectionate towards any white person. It was relieving to hear her speak of him that way. "So what does he do for a living?" I asked. Slowly she began to rock in her chair and said "Nothing. He comes from an extremely rich family. When his parents passed away he and his brother split millions of dollars between the two of them then parted ways. He says his brother used his portion of his money to start his own plantation. His brother's decision split them up for years. Their parents never owned slaves so it was surprising to

Ron to discover his brother's plans. It outraged Ron that he would do such a thing. He couldn't very well cut him off completely but they could never be as close as they were ever again. He doesn't speak of him much and I don't ask. But to answer your question more specifically, now he mostly makes his money by loaning his and collecting an interest. If you can't pay on time he sends me to collect it for him and I'm gonna get that money. You can best believe it because if he doesn't get paid then I don't get paid." Although I knew that she meant every word and was as serious as could be, I couldn't help for laughing a little. "So what about the woman you killed the other day? You can't collect money from a dead person." I asked. Before she could respond, I heard the raspy voice of Mr. Langford say "Well you see, that was more personal than anything. She stole from me. We had a lovely evening together and in the morning I woke up to find that she and my poker winnings from the riverboat were both gone. I saw her again later that day and inquired about my money. She spat in my face in front of a crowd of people and accused me of being a drunken liar that was trying to blame her for my own negligence. She created such a scene that at the moment all I could do was wipe my face and walk away. After that it was time for her to meet Bella." He had the same look of accomplishment on his face when he spoke of Bella that she had when she talked about the guns she brought back for Moses.

"So are you two lovebirds going to sit out here on the porch and talk about me all day or Bella are you going to come inside and tell us what you found out? And Moses is going to love the guns. He's been practicing all day." Mr. Langford said as he turned and waddled back inside. We both laughed and followed him inside of the house. Moses was sitting on the floor with a book in his hand when we walked in. He quickly jumped to his feet and ran to us both with the book. His eyes were blinking fast and he was grinning from ear to ear. He held the small book up to us and turned to the first page. He said "Mr. Langford says he will teach me to read. He already showed me some words." His excitement was well understood. Although I had been reading since I was a child, it was heartwarming to see a grown man so excited over the opportunity of learning to read. "That's good news big man. I told you you're free now. You can do whatever the hell you want to do. I will help Mr. Langford teach you. And look at what Bella got for you." I said as I handed him the bag of guns. He grabbed the bag and looked inside. He held his head up to look Bella in her eyes and asked "Is this for me?" With a smile on her face she nodded her head and said "Yes those are for you. Like Cody said, you're free now and if anyone tries to take your freedom away from you give them both barrels." He reached inside of the bag then pulled out the guns and the gun belt allowing the bag to drop to the floor. Moses handed me the guns so that he could quickly strap on the belt. I handed him his guns back once he had adjusted his belt to fit. He held both guns up to his face and the evilest grin formed on his face as though he had become possessed by Satan himself. He kissed the barrel of both guns and said "Don't you worry none Ms. Bella. Ain't nobody taking nothing from me again, ESPECIALLY my freedom!" Moses slammed the guns into their holsters then turned to Bella and gave her a huge bear hug. The moment was broken up when Mr. Langford blurted out "For crying out loud! It's not getting any earlier. Can you let us know what you found out already?" The three of us laughed and took a seat at the table with Mr. Langford.

We sat at the table while Bella described the layout of the gun shop and the best point of entry.

We all agreed that the best time to break in was at night, the later the better. It would give the mayor's party time to get in full swing. Most of the people attending will be full of alcohol and celebrating. So our chances of being caught were low. We spent the better part of the day planning everything out. Moses was to kick in the back door of the shop to let Bella and I in to grab as many guns and bullets as possible. Mr. Langford was to keep watch from across the street. By midnight we were all headed to town. Just as we suspected, the town was so quiet that it almost appeared to be abandoned. We took our positions as planned. Bella, Moses and I went to the backdoor and let ourselves inside. The wooden door was no match for Moses' large foot and powerful leg. With one blow the door flew open in lightning speed ripping the top hinge clean out of the door frame. Bella and I didn't waste any time running in. Bella had been in the store earlier when she got Moses' guns.

She knew exactly where to go. The shop was pretty dark inside but the outside light coming in through the large window was enough for us to see what we needed. Without hesitation Bella rushed over to a ring of keys hanging on a wall by a nail. She ran behind the counter to open a door that led to the shop's storage room. I stood by the window to see if anyone was coming while Bella found the right key to let us in. Once she was in I rushed inside with her. I had never seen so many guns in one place. The walls were lined with shelves that had all kinds of pistols and rifles. Guns on the left, ammunition on the right and the back wall held the explosives. I filled two sacks with guns and Bella filled her sack with ammunition. I also took the time to grab a few sticks of dynamite before we ran out of the room. Little did we know that while we were on the inside robbing the place, Mr. Langford spotted a man walking up to the shop. He yelled out to the man "Hey you there. Do you happen to know how to get to the party for the mayor?" His loud raspy voice echoed through the empty streets. I ran to the window to see what was going on. Mr. Langford was staggering out into the middle of the street to stop the guy by pretending to be an annoying drunk looking for the party. He caught up with the man just as the fellow was stepping onto the porch of the shop. He was so close that if we had made any noise he surely would have heard one of us. I motioned to Bella to be still and not to say anything. I peeked my head from around the wall to look out of the window. I caught a glimpse of the man's face just before Mr. Langford quickly threw his arm around the guy's shoulder and spun him around to prevent him from seeing me as well. The more the man struggled to get away the more Mr. Langford staggered and pulled him back away from the shop. They made it all of the way back off of the porch and almost to the middle of the street. In a loud drunken slur I heard Mr. Langford say "Do you…do yoooou know the mayor? He's a fine man. I can introduce you to him. Just come with me." The man was so annoyed with Mr. Langford that he finally yelled "SIR! Get your hands off of me and get a hold of yourself. Now I do not have time for you and your drunken babble. And if you will excuse me I have to get something from inside of my shop." He snatched away from Mr. Langford's grasp and headed back towards the shop. By the time he got back to the front door of the shop we were almost to our horses. Just as we were mounting our horses, from a distance we could hear the man in the shop screaming to the top of his lungs "HELP! HELP! I'VE BEEN ROBBED! SOMEONE HELP!" His cries for help went unanswered and we went undiscovered. "What about Mr. Langford?" I asked. Bella smiled and answered "You don't have to worry about Ronald. Trust me, he's ok." For some reason I didn't doubt her. The old man seemed quicker on his feet than he appeared. "I wonder why the shop owner was coming back." Moses asked. Again Bella smiled then reached inside of her bag and said "He was probably coming back for this. It has 'Congratulations Mayor' written on it. He must have forgotten to take it with him." She was holding a small gift wrapped box that was obviously meant to be a gift to the mayor. The owner was coming back to get it for the mayor. We had a quick little laugh then raced out of town with our bags filled and horses galloping at top speed, escaping under the cover of darkness. We managed to pull off the first of many jobs without anyone being the wiser. It was the beginning of a lifetime commitment to each other.

Chapter 15

Time To Hit The Trail

In the morning Bella, Moses and I were awakened by loud knocks on the door. When Bella and I walked out of her bedroom we found Moses standing at the door with Mr. Langford. "Top of the morning everyone!" Mr. Langford yelled out with a huge smile on his face. Bella looked him up and down then said to him "Well it's about damn time! You're getting slow old man." Then she walked back into the bedroom and closed the door behind her. I looked at the closed door then back at Moses and Mr. Langford then the three of us burst out laughing. Bella and I laid back down to get more sleep but it didn't last very long before the sounds of Moses and Mr. Langford out back having more target practice. The sound of gunfire made Bella spring up from the bed. "What in the hell?" she shouted looking around as if we were

181

under attack. I giggled at her startled reaction. She quickly turned her attention to me and said "Oh that's funny huh? I almost had a heart attack and you think it's funny." Then she smacked me in the face with her pillow and jumped on top of me. We rolled around from one end to the other laughing and fondling each other. She made me feel like a kid again. I hadn't felt so carefree since losing my family. The playful wrestling ended with me on top of her pinning her hands to the bed above her head. We stared deeply into each other's eyes until it was as though our souls connected. I could feel the love pouring out through her hands, her eyes and everywhere that our bodies met. Our lips met for a kiss that I couldn't help for traveling to her neck, to her breast, to her naval and then a knock at the door. "WHAT?" Bella yelled at the door. It was Mr. Langford and his poor timing. "Are you two going to lie in bed and bump bellies all day? We need to get going. With all of these guns and things those horses are going to need a break by nightfall. And I want to be there in time to find a spot to camp before they collapse on us." he yelled back from the other side. Bella yelled back "I don't give a..." I covered her mouth with my hand before she could finish because he was right. The last thing we needed was worn out horses in case we needed to get away fast. I took my hand from over her mouth and told her "We have all of the time in the world for this but he's right. Besides, I'm not going anywhere. We met for a reason and I'm excited to see where life takes us from here." She smiled harder than I had ever seen and said "I've been waiting for a man like you for all of my life." We began to kiss again and again Mr. Langford began to bang on the door. "If you knock on that door one more time old man...I swear to God!" Bella screamed. "We're getting up!" I hollered to keep him from knocking again. "You owe me mister!" Bella jokingly advised me but was also serious.

We went ahead and got dressed so that we could help pack some things for our trip. Bella and I stepped outside and were both shocked to find six horses strapped to a stagecoach. Mr. Langford hopped out with his arms wide opened and yelled "SURPRISE!" Bella shook her head and said "I would ask but after all of these years I've learned that sometimes it's best not to know." Once we had everything loaded into the stagecoach Mr. Langford took his place in the driver's seat. Moses and I mounted our horses while Bella slowly walked out of the front door. She stepped down from the porch then turned to face the old small house. She lowered her head as though she knew as I did when I left my hut that it was the last time that she may ever see it again. Finally she gathered herself and blew a kiss to the house then joined us on her own horse. We rode off and I watched Bella looking back at the house that she called home one last time. We decided to stay away from the main roads to prevent any unnecessary run-ins with the law. We took a route that Moses suggested. It was one of the many dark trails that he told us about. We rode for almost three hours before we came up on a cleared out stretch of land with a huge pond nearby. "This should be a good spot for us to camp out for the night. There's plenty of fish in that pond over yonder. But it's best we stay out of sight as much as possible. The house is just on the other side of those trees past the pond." Moses suggested. Even with the company of Mr. Langford, Moses was right. None of us had any papers to prove our freedom which could have proven hard to explain why one old white man was in the woods alone with three blacks and a stagecoach full of weapons. It was a risk we all wanted to avoid. There wasn't a lawman alive dumb enough not to figure out that we were up to something. So we found a spot in the woods and setup camp for the night. Moses and I went to the pond together while Bella and Mr. Langford built a fire for the fish and two tents for sleeping.

After filling up on the fish we caught, the four of us sat down around the campfire and went over our plan. That night we were treated to the surprising and angelic singing voice of Moses. He sang spiritual songs of hope that the field hands would chant while working. His deep melodic voice was as soothing as a mother's hug. We were so entranced by his voice that we didn't realize that we weren't the only audience Moses was entertaining. "It...is you!" rang out over the sounds of the sound of footsteps rustling through the high patches of grass. We all turned to see where the voice was coming from and discovered that we had been spied on by a young black man. His clothes were old and filthy. It was no doubt that they were signs of an overworked field hand.

He rushed over to us with his arms stretched wide open. Moses sprung to his feet to embrace him with his much larger arms. But when Moses' arms wrapped around him the young man's knees buckled. He winced in agony as his face balled up with pain. Moses stepped back arms length from him to take a look at him. "Jordan, what's wrong with you boy? Are you ok?" Moses asked the young man. Jordan broke down to his knees and began to weep like a child. He fell forward exposing an all too familiar large, dark red stain covering the back of his shirt. The shredded shirt was the result of the work from a horse whip wielded by the hands of evil. "It was Jacob. He has been acting like a mad man since you been gone. Yesterday he accused me of not working hard enough. I's was doing as much as I's could but it's hard when there's nothing in yo belly." Jordan explained with tears and fear in his eyes. Moses got down on his knees with Jordan and held him

187

by his shoulders. The tears began to build up in Moses' eyes. "I's couldn't take it no mo Moses. He was gone kill me next time. I knows it. He only stopped because Ms. Hannah told him they needed all the hands they's had on the count of you being dead and all. But I know'd they's was lying. They always do! So when everyone was good and sleep I ran." Jordan continued. "Hannah told everyone that I was dead?" Moses asked then let Jordan go and stood to his feet. He began to pace back and forth holding his head. "What about my wife Maye? Is she ok? My baby girl Asha thinks her daddy is dead. I have to see them and let them see that I'm alive and ok." Moses was so full of rage that he attempted to take off running, running for revenge. I stopped him before he could get going. "Hold up there big man. We only have one shot at this. We have to be smart and stick to the plan. Jordan is actually just what we needed to get in touch with the others to let them know to get ready." I advised him.

Once I was able to get Moses calmed down we all agreed that it would be best that we send Jordan back to the plantation to alert the other slaves that we were coming. Bella cleaned up Jordan's wounds and I found some of the plants that we used for healing in the tribe. I rubbed his back with the plant oil to ease the pain a little. When we finished fixing him up Jordan didn't hesitate to accept the job, for he too was full of rage and revenge for himself as well as for Moses. With his instructions from Moses on who to alert and which ones to tell about the guns, Jordan was off to head back to the hell he had just escaped. We sent him with a bag of loaded pistols to hide until it was time to use them. We watched Jordan take off running through the trees and he soon disappeared in the night like a ghost. Everyone else went back to take their seats around the campfire. I was frozen still in my boots at the bravery of Jordan. I stood looking out to the path he took. I couldn't help for thinking just how much it took for him to turn around and go back to the place he hated. He was taking the risk of being caught. I prayed that he had not yet been discovered missing by Jacob or any of the others. I soon felt the gentle touch of Bella's hand on my shoulder. She asked "What's on your mind honey?" I lowered my head then held it high to the night sky and questioned "Why are we the ones that have to be slaves? Why do our people have to always be the ones in chains? Who said that the white man is the one chosen to rule over everyone?" I looked back down at Bella and asked "Look at what the white man has done and doing. They're killing off as many Indian tribes as possible. They put us in chains then treat us worse than the pig that sleeps in its own shit. They have deemed themselves as masters and overseers of all humans." I gritted my teeth and said "They need to feel some of the pain that they are inflicting. They are the ones that should be in chains for all that they have done! They need to feel the crack of the whip across their backs; the restless and hungry nights! They are NOT masters! I will show them!" Bella wrapped her arms around my trembling body and softly said "You truly are the man that I've been waiting for."

Chapter 16

The Take Over

The four of us were awake and ready to go just before sunrise. We didn't waste much time as we were all eager to get to the plantation to handle our business. It didn't take very long to get to the huge house. We reached the edge of the woods and the house was within view from the tree line surrounding the field worked by the slaves. We took a moment to go over our plans again. Then Bella, Moses and I let Mr. Langford head towards the house as we took off through the cover of the trees to get to the back of the house as we planned. From behind the trees we watched Mr. Langford taking the stagecoach up to the big house. He was met by two men on horses that stopped him only feet away from the high sitting front porch. We were unable to hear what was being said but Moses recognized the two of them immediately. "Is one of them Jacob?" I asked Moses. "No but that's his son Travis getting off of the horse heading into the house. He's Jacob's only child. His pride and joy. He loves that boy more than life itself." It didn't take long before a tall skinny white man walked back out of the house with Travis. "That's Jacob!" Moses stated as the hate became noticeable on his face. The two of them stood on the porch looking out at Mr. Langford. Travis pointed out towards Mr. Langford to apparently inform Jacob of the purpose of the stranger's visit. The two of them walked off of the porch and up to the stagecoach. Jacob walked all around the stagecoach and peeked in its window to inspect for other passengers I assumed. He walked back to the front of the stagecoach and Mr. Langford extended his hand to Jacob for a shake. Jacob just stood there with both of his hands on his hips. Jacob turned to Travis and sent him back to the house. He then looked over at the other guy and motioned for him to go about his business as well. Jacob then stuck his hand out and finally shook Mr. Langford's hand. Soon after that two white women stepped out onto the porch with Travis. "There's Hannah and her mother Scarlett." Moses advised us. The three of them walked up to the stagecoach to meet Mr. Langford. He tipped his hat to the two ladies then stepped down from the stagecoach. He walked around to the door of the coach and opened it. Mr. Langford pulled out his oversized jewel chest and sat it on the ground. When he opened it the two women began to clutch each other's hands and smile from ear to ear. Scarlett turned to Jacob and wrapped her arms around his neck. I don't know what she said to him but she released Jacob and grabbed Mr. Langford by the hand then headed towards the house leaving the chest on the ground behind them. Jacob pointed to the chest and Travis quickly grabbed it up and followed Scarlett into the house.

Jacob and Hannah were still standing in the yard after everyone else had made it into the house. We were about to make our way around to the back of the house when Jacob passionately kissed Hannah in the mouth and smacked her on the ass to send her on her way inside with the others. "Did you see that? Hannah has gotten to Jacob too. We just need to kill all of their sick asses." Moses growled. "No! I have a better idea.

Instead of killing them, we need to do them the way they have been doing black people for centuries." I told the two of them. "What do you mean?" Moses asked. I looked at them and said "What I mean is that shooting and killing them is the easy way out for them. They need to suffer." What do you have in mind?" Bella asked. "Mr. Langford has an old plantation that he has offered to sell me for a small portion of my cut from the money. It's going to need some work and I'm going to need some help. According to Mr. Langford the house already has slave quarters on it. All we need are slaves. I say we take these sick bastards and turn the tables on them. What better way to get the work done and our revenge than to force them into of life of slavery as many of our people are forced to live every day? The life that the two of you were once forced to live. Anyone that are in chains now can either come with me and live as a free man or set out on their own if they choose, especially you and your family Moses. You could be the overseer of them all. But today is the beginning of their end to inflicting pain and suffering on our people. Today they become the slaves and we will become their masters!" Bella looked at me and asked "So what about me? Where do I fit in your plans or did you plan to do all of this without me?" I smiled and answered "Bella there is no way in hell I would even think of doing any of this without the woman of my dreams. Without you none of this would even be possible. I don't just want you to be with me, I NEED you to be with me." She smiled and said "Good answer because I would hate to bust you in the head with the butt of my pistol."

We made our way along the edge of the woods to get in position to meet up with Jordan. The slave quarters sat behind the big house to the left while the overseers' homes were to the right of the big house. We approached from the side of the slave quarters but still had a clear visual of where the overseers lived. It was Sunday so most of the workers had gone home to see their wives and families of their own. Jacob on the other hand was living and raising his son their fulltime after losing his wife to pneumonia when Travis was only six. For the past ten years Travis has been the only family Jacob had left. It was time for us to make our move and for them to pay. We stayed as low as possible to prevent being seen then crept out of the woods and up to one of the slave quarters. Moses gave a coded knock on the back wall of the wooden shack and the exact knock was repeated from the inside. Jordan soon came from inside of the shack and stuck his head around the corner to let us know the coast was clear. Quickly the three of us rushed inside and closed the door before anyone could see us. Inside of the poorly built home were several male slaves waiting to help take down Jacob and whoever was there. Among the group inside were Moses' wife Maye and his daughter Asha. "Daddy!" screamed his daughter as she ran over to give him a big hug. His wife stood in shock with her hands over her mouth and tears of joy pouring from her eyes. Moses released his grip on his daughter and slowly walked towards Maye. She was crying uncontrollably and nearly dropped to her knees when Moses reached out for her. He grabbed her up and pulled her close to him before she could go down. "I didn't think that I would ever see you again." she cried. They hugged and kissed one another as though no one was there but the two of them. I walked up behind Moses and placed my hand on his shoulder then advised him, "As much as I hate to say this…we need to move. We don't have much longer before Mr. Langford is going to make his move. We need to be ready for when he does."

Knowing that time was ticking Moses agreed with me. "Do you have the bag we gave you in here?" I asked Jordan. Without delaying Jordan scurried to the back corner of the shack then kneeled down on one knee. He started pulling up the floor boards then pulled the bag out from underneath the floor. Jordan handed the bag to me then stepped back with a grin that nearly covered his entire face. "Now who other than Jacob and his son are here with them?" I asked. One of the men spoke up and said "Master Franklin, master Overton and Big Jim is the only ones left mister. The rest are gone until tomorrow." I smiled at the idea that there weren't many to deal with. "And does anyone know where those men are now?" I asked. Another guy answered "I saw Master Jacob heading into Big Jim's cabin right before you came knocking. They usually spend most of the day on Sundays over there drinking whiskey and playing cards until they get too drunk to see or walk straight." Before I could say anything another much older grey haired man added "Around nightfall they come looking for our wives and daughters to take away and…" He became so upset at the thoughts of what happens that he couldn't even finish talking. Tears of pain streamed down his face and we were all pained by his emotional words. Maye wrapped her arms around the old gentleman to comfort him. I walked up to them and placed my hand on the man's shoulder and said "They won't be hurting anyone tonight. You have my word on that." The old man held his head up and smiled at me then said "God bless you son." I nodded my head then asked "Have any of you ever held or shot a pistol?" They all looked around at each other to see who would raise their hand or step up but no one ever did. "No problem. You don't have to know how to shoot. All we need is for them to see you all with guns in your hands pointing at them. The three of us will protect you but don't hesitate to pull that trigger if you have to. I don't want to kill them unless it is absolutely necessary." A look of confusion fell across the face of them all. I gave them all a quick rundown on the plans I had to make the overseers slaves and their opportunity to live as free men and women on my future plantation. The news lifted their morale and dried up the tears of the old man.

Chapter 17

The Surprise Attack

Time was running out and we needed to get moving. "Jordan, give all of these men a gun." I instructed. They were like children with candy. I told everyone "Jordan, I need you to go to Big Jim's cabin and tell them that there's a fire at the big house and they need to come right away. When they come running out Bella and I will be on each side of the house waiting for them to get out in the open. I want three of you men to head to the big house to make sure Mr. Langford is ok. Two of you I want to stay here to watch over Maye and Asha. The rest of you I want you to gather up all of the other slaves and let them know that freedom is here but wait until I send for them before they come out. Moses find somewhere to hide until they come outside and we get the drop on them. That's when you can come out and let them see that you are alive and well. But we must act fast." Three of the men set out through the woods to keep from being seen running to the big house as I instructed. Once they were out of sight everyone else took off one at a time to let the others know what we were about to do. Bella and I ran through the woods to come up behind Big Jim's home so that we could get in position. Bella set up on the left and I set up on the right side of Big Jim's small house. I gave Jordan the signal and he jumped right into action. He ran top speed from his shack to Big Jim's place. He began beating on Big Jim's door like a mad man and yelling "HELP! Ms. Scarlett needs help! There's a fire in the kitchen! Come quick!" Just as I planned the four men came bolting out of the house. They all stopped at the same time when Jacob yelled "Wait a minute! I don't see any smoke. What'n the hell is going on here Jordan? There ain't no damn fire is it boy?" They all started to walk back towards Jordan. One of the men appeared to reach for his gun so I left off a shot right at his feet. "What the hell?" the man yelled. They all looked around to find out where the shot came from. That's when Bella and I stepped out into the open pointing two guns each at the group of men. I said "You're right mister. There's no fire…yet. But if you take one more step or even think about reaching for those guns, there will be more smoke than you can handle. I promise you that." Jordan stepped down from Big Jim's porch and stood between Bella and me. "Now my friend Jordan here is going to come over there to remove those firearms from you men. And I suggest that you don't resist and give me a reason to lay one of you down. Not that I would mind killing any of you but I have other plans for you. Now hands up and no sudden moves." I advised them. Jordan walked over and got their guns as I told them and brought them back to me. "Who the hell do you think you are? You don't have plans for me nigger! I will kill you!" one of the men shouted at me. I assumed he was Big Jim considering he was the biggest of the all. I shot him in the face and killed him right where he stood. "Now does anyone else want to threaten the big black man with the gun?" I asked. The remaining three men looked at each other then back at me but never said a word. They knew then that I meant business.

I sent Jordan to go gather up the rest of the slaves and bring them where we were. When Jordan left I told the three men "In a moment we're all going to head up to the big house to talk about this fire Jordan mentioned. Then we're all going on a long trip. But before we do any of that, I have someone that I want you to meet." A look of confusion came across their faces as I let out a high pitch whistle for Moses to come out and show himself. Moses stepped from behind one of the vacant overseer's cabin with hate and a thirst for blood. Even I wouldn't have wanted to tangle with him at that moment but Jacob on the other hand was going to have his hands full. "I believe you all know my other good friend here." I said with a laugh. "One of you killed his boy some time ago and I believe it was you there Jacob. He has been waiting a long time to talk to you about it. You other two, I suggest that you step aside and not get in this. I will not hesitate to lay you next to your friend." I told them. They both stepped away from Jacob as I recommended. Moses walked up to Jacob and stood a few feet away from him then stopped. He took off his gun belt and tossed it in my direction. Jacob dropped his head and smiled then told Moses "You shouldn't have done that. As a matter of fact you shouldn't have ever come back here. Hannah said you were killed by some other slave that they were supposed to be bringing back. She said that he killed everyone but her. I see now that she lied to us all." The two of them started circling each other positioned to pounce at any time they were ready. Jacob continued with "I thought you died trying to save Richard's life. That's the only reason I didn't let the boys have Asha. But I'm going to tear you a new asshole...just like I did Asha. I kept her young body for myself! And she was worth the wait. What is she now thirteen or fourteen...somewhere around there? Fresh and tender like I like em. She fought like a wildcat and much noisier of a piece of tail than Maye's old ass. Now she did meet all of the boys." Moses had heard enough. I sent

Jordan to go get the rest of the slaves. They came to join us just as Moses lunged for Jacob and caught him around his neck with both hands. Everyone including Maye and Asha circled around the two men to watch the hand to hand battle. Jacob tripped Moses and they both stumbled to the ground forcing Moses to lose his grip as they rolled in the dirt. They both quickly hopped to their feet with their fists up and ready. Jacob rushed in with his head down to grab Moses by the waist but was met with a massive right upper cut that stood him straight up. Surprisingly Jacob took it like a champ until Moses' immediate left jab sent teeth and blood flying from Jacob's mouth. He somehow managed to deliver a crushing jab of his own that split open Moses' left eyebrow. The gushing blood from Moses poured into his eye making it hard to see the left right combination from Jacob. Moses stepped back to wipe the blood from his eye and noticed that his family was standing there watching. In a fit of rage Moses let out a cry reminiscent of an angry bear then charged Jacob. In no time he had Jacob held high above his head and slammed his body into the hard ground. Moses came down on top of Jacob unleashing a flurry of haymakers that left Jacob squirming unsuccessfully to get from underneath Moses' large body. His attempts to break free and get away were useless. Moses straddled Jacob and blow after blow he pounded Jacob until his face and hair were soaked in blood.

Moses had beaten Jacob unconscious and was not planning on stopping until I yelled out "That's enough. Remember we need him." My words stopped Moses in motion with his large powerful fist raised high and on its way down to pound Jacob's bloody face. Moses lowered is fist and stood to his feet then spit in Jacob's face. Without warning Moses drew his pistol and pointed it straight at Jacob's face. "Moses!" Maye yelled and slowly started walking towards him. His hand was shaking more than a leaf in a windstorm. "You don't have to do this. If we follow Cody's plan, Jacob will spend the rest of his days paying for ALL of the evil he's done, they will all pay! Now PLEASE put the gun down." Maye begged but her words were falling on deaf ears. Moses began to tear up as he pulled back the hammer on his pistol, preparing to end the life of Jacob. "DADDY NO!" Asha cried out. She ran over to her parents to beg Moses to spare Jacob. "She's seen plenty of evil in her short lifetime already. Do NOT become a part of the hatred that she will remember in her life." Maye pleaded with him. Asha placed her hand on Moses' hand with the gun and gradually guided his hand and the pistol down to his side. Moses released the gun and allowed it to fall to the ground near his feet. He broke down to his knees and cried uncontrollably. Maye and Asha hugged him together for a moment then helped him back to his feet. They began to walk back to Bella and me, leaving Jacob lying on the ground motionless. Before they made the short walk to us Asha ran back to Jacob and stomped him as hard as she could in his nuts. The stomp awakened Jacob and he rolled over on his side clutching his crotch with both hands. He let out a cry of pain that echoed across the plantation grounds. Asha quickly picked up the pistol Moses left behind and raised the barrel then aimed it at Jacob. He held his hand out as though it could shield him from the bullet. Instead of shooting him, Asha turned and ran as fast as she could to us. I motioned to Jordan to come to me. I asked him "How many horses are here?" The look of confusion on his face made me realize that he didn't know because he couldn't count. "Do you know the names of the horses?" He held his head down in shame and said "Yesuh!" I raised his chin up with my hand and told him "Hey...the days of being shamed are over. It's not your fault. You were made this way because the white man knows that if blacks learn to read, write and count that their days of ruling us will be numbered. Don't you worry. I'm going to make sure everyone of you learn how to do all of that. I will teach you myself. Now just tell me the names of each horse and I will know how many there are here." He looked up at me and gave me a big smile then named thirteen horses. I told him "You did great young man. Now have someone to hitch the horse to those covered wagons I saw on the side of the horses stable. Then tie up those two over there and get that piece of shit Jacob too. Put them in wagons and make sure they don't get away. Let everyone get only the things that are most important to them because we're going to set fire to everything. Me, Bella and Moses are headed to the big house to finish up our business before we leave. When we get done we will meet you all back here to burn this bitch DOWN!" When I said that, the air became filled with an outcry of cheers from all of the slaves.

Chapter 18

Burning Down The House

When we got to the big house Mr. Langford and the three men that I sent had Travis, Scarlett and Hannah all sitting under gunpoint on a couch in the library of the home. Mr. Langford was sitting in a chair behind a large and extremely expensive looking desk with a tea cup in his hand. The three men were standing directly in front of the three and ready to pull their triggers with the first opportunity. I told them they could go join the others and we will be there soon. I advised them to find Jordan so that he could tell them what to do. They quickly ran out of the house to find Jordan as

I suggested. "What are you doing?" Bella asked Mr. Langford. "What does it look like I'm doing? You three took so long that I got thirsty. Hannah was kind enough to fix me a cup of tea to go with their exquisitely expensive whiskey. Someone around here has much better taste in drinks than their home décor. Some of the pieces in here are just hideous!" he responded with a look of disgust for their house furniture. Hannah jumped up from her seat and yelled "KISS MY ASS! You MADE me fix you tea!" Bella drew her pistol and yelled back at Hannah "SIT your ass back down! Right now." Hannah was in no rush to be blown away so she did as she was told and took a seat. Then Bella turned her attention back to Mr. Langford. "That's not what I'm talking about. You old fart. Did you find the money?" she barked. He took a sip from his cup and said "Well of course I did." Then he took another sip. My patience was beginning to wear thin. I yelled out "So where is it?" He pointed to a large black safe in the corner across the room. It was about five and a half feet tall with a large wheel and handle attached to the door. "Unless you are as good at safe cracking as you are at shooting, it's going to stay in there because they're not telling us the combination." Mr. Langford said. Then he took yet another sip of his tea and crossed his legs.

"Well they have to do something." I said. Bella joined in with "You have that right. I didn't give up everything I have to come this far for nothing. We're not leaving here empty handed. So one of you better get to talking and fast." Bella started slowly walking over to the couch where the three of them were sitting. She got directly in front of Hannah then turned to Mr. Langford and asked "Did you try whooping some ass?" He chuckled and answered "Oh heavens no. You know that I would never hit a woman." Bella glanced over at the bloody lip Hannah was nursing and said "So how did her lip get busted? You mean to tell me that you can hit her for some damn tea but not for some money? Are you crazy?" He continued to sip his tea then said "Don't be absurd. I let one of the other men slap her. He got way more satisfaction from it than I ever could. Like I said, I could never hit a woman." Bella giggled a little and said "You might can't hit a woman but I can." When she turned her attention back to Hannah she brought the back of her right hand and pistol down across Hannah's face. Blood shot from Scarlett's eyelid and splattered all over Travis' face and shirt. Hannah cried out in pain and Travis pissed his pants. Bella's hand was on its way back down for another face crushing blow when Scarlett yelled out "WAIT! PLEASE! We don't know the combination. Richard bought the safe almost a year ago. He never told anyone the combination and now he's dead. We sent a wire to the company that made it but they said it could be weeks before they could get someone out here to open it." Bella stared into Hannah's eyes then said "I don't believe you." She raised her hand again and Scarlett screamed "It's the truth. I swear! The only other way to get it open is to use dynamite to blow it open." I smiled and said "Well hell, why didn't you say so in the first place. You might could have saved your daughter from getting her eye split open. Although seeing that she was planning on killing you herself, the whole thing seems a bit ironic. Don't you think?" The look of shock on Scarlett's face was priceless. She had no idea that Hannah was planning to kill her all along. I sent Moses outside to get two sticks of dynamite from my horse. I stuck one stick in between the handle and the other between the wheel and the door. "Alright we need to go outside. I don't think we need to be in here when this thing blows." I suggested. Moses looked at me and asked "Don't you need to light them?" I laughed a little then put my hand on his large shoulder and said "Hell no. I'm not staying in here to light them, Travis is. And if he doesn't do it, I'm going to blow a hole in his chest big enough to put even your hand through it." We looked back over at Travis together then even more piss began to soak through the couch and onto the floor.

We all went outside while Travis stayed behind to light the dynamite sticks. It didn't take long for Scarlett to confront Hannah about her plot to kill her. "What did he mean when he said that you were planning on killing me?" Scarlett asked Hannah. An obvious look of disgust instantly fell across Hannah's face. Scarlett gasped at Hannah's facial expression of admitted guilt. "So it's true? After all that I've done for you? That's what you planned to do to ME?" Scarlett cried out. Her face was beet red and covered in tears of betrayal. "Why? Hannah why would you want to do such a thing?" Scarlett continued questioning. "Your stepfather and I…" Scarlett started saying but she was abruptly interrupted by Hannah's outcry of her own. "You and my stepfather? You allowed him and his brother to treat me like a common two bit whore. And you sat back doing nothing to stop it! You KNEW what they were doing to me. You are no MOTHER!" Hannah then turned and looked at the four of us and pointed at Bella then said "This is all your fault. If you hadn't somehow saved them in the saloon then none of this would be happening. Everything was perfect. Jacob and I wouldn't have had to kill Moses after I was done using him. It was better than Jacob and I planned it. In a few days I would have had the combination to the safe and headed out of town to start a new life with Jacob. But you two niggers had to ruin it. You think you're so tough. You ain't SHIT without that gun in your hand. Put it down and I will… beat… your… ASS!" Just then we all heard the sound of boots stomping and running on the front porch. It was Travis making a mad dash out of the house and jumping off of the porch. The loud sounds of the dynamite rang out from inside of the big house. Travis fell to the ground and rolled a couple of times before he came to a complete stop.

Travis stood to his feet and looked back towards the house as though he couldn't believe he was still alive. The laughter from Mr. Langford puzzled us all. "What's so funny? I could have been killed in there!" Travis shouted at the old man. He appeared as though he wanted to lunge for Mr. Langford until he felt the barrel of my gun digging into the bottom of his chin to put an immediate halt to whatever he thought he was going to do. "If you take one more step you will die...right out here." I told him. He made the wise decision to stay put and not move a muscle. Mr. Langford laughed even harder and said "You dumb ass. They wouldn't have killed you unless you stood directly in front of the blast. You could have simply gone into the other room to avoid any serious harm. We came out here to avoid the loud BOOM!" In his unique waddle of a walk the old man headed back to the house still laughing at Travis. "You fellas go right ahead inside. Hannah and I are going to stay out here and have a little 'girl' talk." Bella said to us while she and Hannah glared at each other. "Hey, stay out here and keep an eye on them." I said to Moses. Bella waved Moses off and said "Oh no! No need for that. This won't take long at all baby. I'll be finished by the time you all come out. Umm hmm!" Bella handed her guns to Mr. Langford then started walking towards Hannah. Hannah balled up her fist and began to meet Bella. As bad as I wanted to watch, I also knew that we needed to be getting out of there in case someone heard the blast and came to be nosey. "Well grab Scarlett and let's go get this money." I told Moses. Moses grabbed Scarlett by the arm and led her towards the house. "Aren't you coming? I don't think she needs us for this." I suggested to Mr. Langford. He looked at me with a sly grin and said "Oh I know that she doesn't need us just as you don't need me in there. The four of you can handle that. I have satchels in my jewel chest that you can use to put the money in. You'll find it on the floor next to the chair I was sitting in but I'm not missing this my dear man. And she can't make me leave. So go ahead and hurry. I'll be here when you get back. Be sure to bring the chest out with you. I don't want to leave it behind" I grabbed Travis and started heading inside with Moses and Scarlett. Before we could make it to the steps of the porch I heard Bella say "Come here BITCH!" I turned back around just in time to see Bella give Hannah a left jab and right hook before Hannah could get a swing in. I was satisfied with knowing that Bella could take care of herself without a guns as well.

We walked back into the library and found that the door had been blown clean off of the safe. It was lying on the floor next to the safe. The safe was pretty much destroyed but the money was completely unharmed. We found Mr. Langford's chest and filled three large satchels with huge stacks of money wrapped in bands from the bank. It was more money than I had ever seen at one time. From the look on Scarlett's face it was obvious that she was just as clueless to how much money was in there as the rest of us. Once we cleaned out the safe we filled two more satchels with all of their expensive silverware and many other valuables around the house. Before leaving out for good we set a fire in each room downstairs. By the time we came out, the house was almost too smoky to see clearly. When we got to the porch Bella and Mr. Langford were standing there waiting for us like she said and Hannah was lying on the ground bloody and unconscious. We got

Hannah off of the ground and we all headed back to meet up with the others back at the slave quarters. When we got there they had done everything that I asked and were patiently waiting for our return. They began to cheer when the thick smoke from the big house began to roll out of the windows and doors as the fire consumed the massive home. I gathered everyone together and reminded them that they had the option of coming with me or going off on their own. Not one single person chose to go by themselves. I went ahead and gave Jordan the ok to burn the rest of the quarters so that we could begin our new journey. While everyone rushed off to set fire to the other homes I pulled Mr. Langford to the side for a quick talk. "When I got the satchels from your chest I noticed a stack of papers. What were those?" I asked. "Oh yes. I almost forgot about those. While I was waiting for you to get to the big house I stumbled across an inventory list of slaves they owned. You see, after you told me your plans to free the slaves on this plantation. I had freedom papers printed while I was in town last. That's what took me so long for me to get back that morning after the gun shop. I had Scarlett to sign papers for each one of the names on the list. Should you ever need them, there are papers in there for you and Bella as well." I shook the old man's hand and thanked him. When everyone got back from setting their fires we loaded up and headed to the woods. We had five covered wagons that we used to hide our new slaves and money in case we were spotted or stopped. Bella and I rode on the money wagon with Mr. Langford and Moses rode with Maye and Asha on their own wagon. With Mr. Langford sitting in front of our wagon train, it would appear that he was simply moving to a new home and transporting his slaves. As long as we covered the faces and hands of everyone in the back of the wagon when needed, then no one could tell that we had white people mixed in with the others that appeared to be cargo as well. Just before we pulled off from the burning plantation, Mr. Langford looked over at me and said "You do know that we're going to need more than just five slaves to fix up the place I'm selling you right?" I smiled and said "Absolutely. There's a whole world full of them out there. We just have to go get them." He smiled then leaned back in his seat on the wagon and said "And I know just where to find the right ones." The three of us laughed then pulled off to lead everyone on one of the many dark trails to start a new life for us all.

To be continued...

www.ingramcontent.com/pod-product-compliance
Lightning Source LLC
Chambersburg PA
CBHW020315260626
47156CB00004B/1232